FOREVER SERIES 🐚 BOOK 2

A HATTERAS *Surprise*

HOPE TOLER DOUGHERTY

Scrivenings PRESS
Quench your thirst for story.
www.ScriveningsPress.com

Published by Scrivenings Press LLC
15 Lucky Lane
Morrilton, Arkansas 72110
https://ScriveningsPress.com

Printed in the United States of America

Paperback ISBN 978-1-64917-228-0

eBook ISBN 978-1-64917-229-7

Cover by Linda Fulkerson - www.bookmarketinggraphics.com

For all the people who help me tell my stories, especially Jeff Radford who helped me with fishing tournaments and boat details, Earl W. Worley, Jr., Chief Operating Officer of KS Bank who answered banking questions, and Walt Wolfram, PhD, William C. Friday Distinguished University Professor and Director of the Language & Life Project at NC State University who spent an engaging half hour discussing the Hoi Toide dialect with me. It takes a village, and I'm indebted to many gracious people. Thank you!

CHAPTER 1

For a moment, Ben Daniels was fifteen again. The tackle shop matched exactly the one in his memory. The same weathered planks. The same signs for bait and ice. A side portion had been added, but the front cast him back to ice cream cones and Popsicles with his siblings on melting afternoons.

"This is it. Nice job, man." Talking out loud. To himself. Must be more tired than he thought.

He exited his car to stretch as scenes from that long ago summer vacation flooded his head—climbing the Hatteras Lighthouse, riding the waves, and a little girl with blond braids who tagged along or, rather, led them on other adventures.

What was her name? Would she, like the tackle shop, still be here?

He smiled and shut his door, a refreshing breeze blowing off the sound. The extended weather report promised more temperate days like this one on the Outer Banks for the remainder of October. Fantastic. He rolled his shoulders and headed inside.

A beach music favorite he recognized from college greeted

him along with a woman sporting cropped gray hair. "Good afternoon. What can we help you with today?" She turned from a rod and reel display and moved to the cash register.

"Hey." He blinked, pulling himself to the present. "I'm looking for a beach cottage."

"For rentals, Island Realty is back up the road a bit." The woman jerked her head toward the way he'd just come.

"No, ma'am, I'm staying at the Teachy Bed and Breakfast. I'm looking for the cottage my family rented years ago. I don't have the address, but it's near this store."

"When we talkin', sonny?"

"2000 or so."

"Pretty good chance the cottage is gone by now. Storms, rebuilding, and such."

"Sure. I wanted to find it for old time's sake. It was a special place, a special time for my family."

A door behind the counter opened, and a woman with sandy blond hair stepped into the shop. He sucked in a breath.

"Hazel, do you have—" she froze in the doorway, a deer caught in a flood light. She dragged her wide eyes from his, muttered, "Excuse me," and vanished into the back room.

"That's too bad. Ahm." He glanced at the office door, squinting his eyes. A crazy idea lit in his mind. "I'm also looking for someone I met back then. Someone named Ginny?" The name popped out of his mouth before he could question it. "Do you know her?"

An eyebrow arced to Hazel's gray hair, and she stiffened like a momma bear growling in front of her den. "Maybe. Maybe not. Who wants to know?"

Ben glanced again at the door and offered his hand across the counter. "I'm Ben Daniels. I think you know her, and I think she's in that office."

She clasped his hand in a firm grip, warning of a strong will. "If that's true, why did she turn around when she laid eyes on

2

you? Why doesn't she want to see you? Are you that fellow from N.C. State? The one who broke her heart?" She raked her almost-black eyes over him and back again.

"No, ma'am. When we vacationed here, she showed us around the island. I'd love to say hello. That's all." He smiled, hoping his eyes crinkled like his sister teased him about. Would charm work on this fierce gatekeeper? "She's in the office, right?"

"She must not recognize you since she closed the door." Hazel slid a small pumpkin closer to the cash register and flattened her palms on the counter, leaning toward him. "Or maybe she did recognize you. Just doesn't want to talk to you."

Buckling under her guilt-inducing gaze, he grabbed onto the first excuse. "It's been around twenty years. She probably forgot some tourists here for just one week." He raised his eyebrows. "Do you mind if I knock and say hello?'

Hazel studied him and consented on her terms. "I'll knock and see if she's busy."

～

GINNY CLICKED the door closed and leaned against it, blowing out a raggedy breath. Old humiliation blanketed her. Twenty-year-old humiliation with ample doses of worthlessness and betrayal pressed on her shoulders. Ben. After all these years.

If he isn't Ben, he's a dead ringer. He's taller, more filled out. His voice is deeper, but his sea green eyes are the same.

Hey, God. That stranger dredged up a memory that makes me feel less than. I know. I know. I'm not that little girl with the hand-me-down bike, the faded shorts, the funny speech. My self-worth comes from You. I know You love me, but I just got blindsided. I need some peace.

The back window showed a tranquil scene of sea oats waving in the breeze, clouds floating over the Pamlico Sound. Three tiny boats sailed on the horizon. The normal island scenes calmed her heart and regulated her breath. Ben. After all these years. She shook her head. Her first crush. Her handsome boy from a far away, great big city—Charlotte. Ben. One of the ones who'd laughed at her behind her back, mocked her speech.

The memory, decades old now, still stung.

Just breathe. The guy would be gone in a few minutes.

Sunlight danced on the waves outside her window, casting her mind to the week for the first time in years. She'd nursed the crush, tainted with humiliation, for years until Matt Tomes asked her to the prom. That relationship lasted until she left for East Carolina University and met a boy from New Jersey who loved her island accent and never made fun of it. To her face at least.

Other guys piqued her interest in subsequent years, but Ben's memory and green eyes hovered in the back of her mind, always a silent yardstick.

Twenty-year-old pictures flickered in her mind from that golden week. Ben, helping her into her boat even though she didn't need it. Praising her island skills. Making her feel like she was sixteen instead of ten. Stirring boyfriend-girlfriend fantasies. Oh, what silly thoughts of a ten-year-old.

Breathe, Ginny. You can show the quarterly reports to Hazel in a few minutes.

As soon as the screen door slams.

A KNOCK JERKED her heart rate into high gear again. Hazel never knocked—even when the door was closed. Not a good sign.

"Yes."

Hazel slid in through a just-big-enough crack in the door and closed it behind her. "Why are you hiding in here?"

"I'm not—"

"You walked out front, saw that man, turned right around,

and shut the door. Why? Is he the jerk who broke your heart in Raleigh?"

"No one—"

"You came back here with your tail between your legs and started keeping the office for your daddy."

"Wrong." Ginny fingered a fishing lure of her father's she kept on his desk. "Daddy passed. The store needed me, and my video project was finished."

"But you hadn't finished your doctorate. Plus, my version's better." Hazel shrugged. "Anyway, he's singing some song about vacationing here a long time ago. Wants to say hey."

Heat climbed up her neck.

So, Ben's back on the island. Remembered her after all these years. Asked for her.

Calm down, heart. Saying hello for a quick minute should be fine. No problem.

God, some help with a problem, please.

Filling her lungs with a good breath, she followed Hazel back into the shop. Her gaze flickered toward his face, fell to a button on his chest. She released the breath and forced her eyes up to meet his. Yep. Same green ones she remembered.

"Hello. Hazel said you wanted to see me."

"Yeah. Ginny, it's good to see you again. Ben Daniels. We met a long time ago when my family stayed in a cottage not too far from here."

"Oh." She smiled. "We get a lot of visitors on the island. I'm sure you can imagine."

Hesitating, Ben tilted his head. "Right, but you showed my family, my two brothers and sister, to some of your haunts. Took us crabbing and ate what we caught for supper with my parents. We climbed the lighthouse together too."

"Oh." Her eyes widened. "Of course, I remember you. Wow. A long time ago. I hope your family's doing well." Did she sound kind and welcoming but non-committal at the same time?

Ginny caught Hazel watching her pleat the hem of her blouse. She smoothed down the creased fabric and stuck her hand in the pocket of her jeans.

"You helped us look for shells too. My sister dreamed of finding a conch shell, but we never did."

"Right. Your sister." Ginny cocked her head. "What was her name?" Josie.

Behind the counter, Hazel coughed twice, then cleared her throat for an exclamation point.

His eyes narrowed. "Josie."

Focusing on him, she refused to look at Hazel. "Josie. Right. It's a shame she didn't get one. I'm usually pretty good at finding shells."

"We heard about her disappointment for months afterward." He grinned at her.

"Oh, no. Well, maybe you can find one for her before you go back to Charlotte." Her stomach dropped. Big mouth. Big mouth.

His head jerked. "You—"

"It's been nice to see you again." Backing toward her office, she felt for the doorknob. "I'm glad you stopped by. Enjoy your stay on the island." She slipped through the crack in the doorway and disappeared.

CHAPTER 2

"*Well*, well, well. You do remember our visitor." Arms crossed in front of her, Hazel leaned against the door frame, daring Ginny to deny it. "Worrying the hem of your shirt gave you away. Uh-huh." She nodded. "It's a telltale sign you're lying, by the way." A smile stretched across her face.

"I don't lie." Ginny rolled her swivel chair back, planning her escape from the determined woman heading her way.

"You were evading the truth. Telling part of it anyway. Then you stuck your foot right in it when you said, 'Charlotte.'" Hazel slapped the desktop and hooted.

Ginny gritted her teeth. "How long until you retire?"

"Never. I'll be a sand burr on your heel for as long as I can figure math in my head."

"The cash register calculates for us." Ginny circled the desk and headed to the front of the store.

"Not when the power goes out."

"Don't bank on family ties to keep your job."

"Speaking of replacements, have you found yours yet? Shoulder season is here and just about gone. We need to train

7

somebody before peak season starts next spring, and you need to get back to Raleigh."

Ginny grimaced. "I'll let you know. And did I overhear you offer my services to show him around the island? I have work to do here. Thank you very much." Ginny straightened a box of Snickers in the glass display case, reminded herself to buy candy for the Trick or Treaters who'd be knocking soon.

"Your daddy left the store to you and," Hazel made a face, "your brother, but you don't have to work here to own it. You're not the only one who can run it."

"Trying to get rid of me?"

"I'm trying to be serious. We haven't talked about Raleigh in a while."

Good reasons too. A bad breakup, a pass-over for lead on a new speech video, and her daddy's funeral ... not interesting topics. Licking her wounds for months at home helped, the island rhythms soothing her raw feelings.

"You're in this office too much. Get out and about. Have some fun. Plus, how're you going to finish your dissertation if you're hiding in here?"

As always, dissertation talk bristled her back. "My project's fine, and anyway he'll have his own vacation plans." She moved a box of promotional keychains to a more prominent place on the counter near the family photo. Mom, Dad, herself with her arm around her big brother's waist. Where are you? Are you okay? Come home and run the store like Daddy—

"Nope. Not here on vacation. He's taking Thumb Nelson's place at the bank. You didn't hear that part when you were eaves-dropping?"

Her breath caught, and her eyes flew to Hazel. "He's moving here?" Too late, she couldn't tamper the curiosity in her voice.

Hazel shot her a gotcha smile. "Temporarily. While they find a permanent manager." An idea animated her face. "Hey. Invite him to church, then go eat at Calmside for the Sunday Special."

8

"I don't think ..." She fiddled with the price tag on a sun visor. Why not help him discover Hatteras? Her social calendar certainly had time for fun excursions, but too much time with this blast from the past could fan the flame of her schoolgirl crush, lighting some serious heartache for her when he returned to Charlotte.

Too many site seeing trips with the handsome bank manager and Hazel would be buying a wedding magazine at the Red and White or saving wedding dress pins on her Pinterest page. Maybe not yet, but the thought would absolutely cross Hazel's mind. She'd already mentioned two different dating apps in the last month and tried to set Ginny up with a new UPS driver. The plan might have worked if not for his wife and twin daughters.

"That boy's new to the island. He needs a guide to show him around, give a little history. Think about it and go finish up. It's almost quittin' time." Hazel shooed Ginny toward the office.

"He's not a boy." He's a grown man with a lovely face and nicely shaped arms and—

"You noticed, did you?"

Ginny slammed the office door on the throaty chuckle coming from her irritating second cousin once-removed, behind the counter. She really needed to get back to Raleigh.

BEN'S LUGGAGE thumped on the floor of the Teachy Bed & Breakfast. The B & B offered an off-season, extended rate, which, of course, made his Charlotte boss happy since the assignment could last several weeks, maybe even months. The job listing would go live sometime in the coming week. How many résumés would flood the listing?

Working in a resort location must be a coveted placement for most people. As remote as Hatteras was, thirty miles into the ocean off the main coast, its beautiful shores enticed people year-round. Or so the pamphlet from the front desk claimed. He dropped the pamphlet and the to-go bag of popcorn shrimp on the bedside table and flopped onto the queen-sized bed like a starfish, releasing a long, road-weary sigh.

The scenic but lengthy drive zapped his physical and mental energy, especially the last sixty miles or so with the three long bridges connecting the mainland to the island. Seven hours in the car made for cramped legs and a crick in his neck. He rolled it to loosen the knots, wincing at the crackle and pops.

He reached for the bag marked with tracings of grease waiting on his bedside table and stabbed the wooden fork into the boat tray of fried shrimp. He speared two at once and crammed them into his mouth. Delicious. Crunchy. Still warm from the takeout grill.

Mental note: *Get a list of the best restaurants the locals frequent from Ginny.* Mental note number two: *Invite Ginny to dinner.* He smiled to himself. Nice mental note.

Stopping by the bait and tackle shop? Genius. Reconnecting with Ginny? An interesting surprise. Could it be more? A friend to re-introduce him to the island would be more than welcome.

He picked up the remote and turned on the TV to a music channel. More stress evaporated with the melody of soft rhythm and blues in the background. Swallowing some orange sports drink, he let his mind return to his family's vacation.

A hazy picture of a pigtailed little girl teased him, parking her bike beside the screened-in porch of the cottage, taking Josie for rides in her Jon boat. Her hair, darker today, swung over her shoulder in a single braid. Her blue eyes still flashed like way back then, but they held a guarded look now. Twenty years ago, she'd warmed up to his family in less than a day, sharing story after story about the island during their excursions. She didn't send the same open vibe today, however.

Listening to her back then fascinated him on two points, the island lore as well as her accent. Ben had heard about the Hoi

Toide speech of the North Carolina coast on TV, but that summer he experienced it firsthand. If the locals spoke too fast, the language almost sounded like a foreign one.

She didn't really have a detectable accent today. Had she lived off the island? Was she trying to speak without any discernible accent?

Grabbing his phone, he punched his sister's number. She answered on the first ring.

"Hey. You left at eight o'clock. You should've been there by three. It's almost six. What gives?"

"Hello to you too. I rode around the island a bit. Trying to get the lay of the land. I'm in my room now." He slipped off his shoes and let them drop to the hardwood floor. "You'll never guess who I saw this afternoon." He stuffed three french fries into his mouth.

"Who?"

"Ginny from Hatteras Island." He arched his foot, enjoying the pull in his calf.

A quick silence filled the line, then a gasp. "Vacation Ginny? What a fierce and funny girl. Just the best. I was so jealous of what she knew how to do. All you boys thought she was fabulous too."

"Yeah, she had skills all right."

"I thought she liked us too. I never understood why she didn't come to our cottage to tell us bye before we left. I had a friendship bracelet for her. Maybe she was too sad to see us go."

He took another swallow. "Maybe she was glad to be rid of us." She didn't seem too happy to see him today. Not really into revisiting memory lane. Very skittish. Cool, in fact.

"Maybe. How'd you find her?"

"I wanted to find the cottage we stayed in." He balled up his napkin and banked it off the back wall into the waste basket. "Remember the bait and tackle shop with the ice cream treats? There she was."

"I'm so happy you found her. Tell her hello if she remembers me. Anyway, when you coming home? You got about two, two and a half months, then Christmas!"

"I just got here, Josie."

"Right. Just wanted you to know you're missed. Plus, your promotion that includes the fancy office is waiting."

"If this assignment goes well, and that's a big if. Sally Grimes is targeting the promotion too." He yawned. "Keep Heath and Sam in line."

"A tough job for a little sister, but you know I will. Come home soon. I need help planning the wedding."

"Ha. You're goofy."

"Just missing my big brother. Hey, a Christmas present from the beach would be really special this year."

"Come home soon with Christmas presents and a promotion. Got it. I'll see what I can do."

CHAPTER 3

*W*as this a good idea?

Ben shifted his car into park in front of Ginny's tackle shop and killed the engine. How much would this new venture set him back? Quick online searches had revealed hefty prices for fancy equipment, but he'd spend his dollars locally, especially if spending them at this local establishment fostered more conversations with Ginny. If the purchase included more chats with the crusty gatekeeper and her beautiful colleague then money well spent, for sure.

Thoughts of Ginny occupied his mind off and on all week. Her mention of Charlotte belied her faulty memory and dismayed her too. Why else would she scramble back to her office the moment the word fell out of her mouth? What did the Charlotte slip up mean? Puzzling. Intriguing even. Maybe learning to fish would lead to a distraction for the island stay and a mystery solved.

Time to feed the local economy.

He cracked open the door, and a bell jingled. The smell of coffee greeted him. Hazel, dressed in an untucked plaid shirt, looked up from, according to his online search, an expensive reel.

"Well, you're back. How was your week on the island? Got any money to lend out? I could use about a pound of twenties." She laughed at her own faded joke.

"I'll let you know if I have any extra. How's that?"

"Don't tease me, son!" She laid down the reel and leaned her hands on the counter. "What can I do for you today?"

"I thought I'd see how the fish were running this morning." He nodded to the reel. "I need a few supplies."

"Is that right?" She hooked her thumbs into the loops of her jeans. "You're a fisherman, are you?"

His eyes wandered to the closed office door. Are you in there, Ginny? "Ah, to tell the truth—"

"I expect you to."

"I guess I'm a learning fisherman." He grinned.

She nodded. "Gotcha. No shame in that. Everybody starts somewhere. You fished at all?"

"Of course."

"With anything other than a cane pole and a cork?"

"Ah." He glanced again at the door.

"Shush." She cut off his answer before he began. "We'll fix you up, buddy. Pier or boat? And what kind of fish you plannin' to catch?"

Raised eyebrows transformed a blank look. "Definitely pier. And big ones?"

Hazel hooted again. "Right. I like a man with confidence. And by the way. Ginny's not here yet."

"Ahh."

"No need to say a thing. Anyway, she's turning in now." Hazel's gaze skirted over his shoulder.

He followed her glance. A bright yellow Jeep crunched on the gravel and rolled past the building.

"She'll be right in." Hazel grinned.

An uptick in his heart rate surprised him. Yes, she's beautiful, but he was here on business, supporting her business, minding his own business. Then why did his heart beat like he'd been caught stealing a candy bar from a checkout line? Yeah, she had impressive skills at ten years old that wowed teen-aged boys, but they were both adults now. He had plenty of successes and skills too. They just didn't include fishing.

Not to mention, his promotion waited for him in Charlotte.

The back door creaked open, and a cinnamon aroma wafted in with Ginny. "Morning, Hazel. Apple Ugly in the house. I got the last one." She froze, a paper bag raised and swinging in her left hand. "Ben."

HER BREATH CAUGHT MID-SENTENCE. Ben. What was he doing here? On a Saturday morning? She placed the bag of gooey, apple-laden pastry near the pot of coffee on the back counter. Hazel prided herself with brewing delicious coffee, and Ginny learned quickly not to bring outside coffee with the morning breakfast treat. She breathed in a long breath of the strong aroma.

Thoughts of him interrupted her concentration all week, but she denied herself trips to the bank. Hazel's knowing eyes detected the ruse forcing her to make the cash deposits, but for once, kept her commentary to herself.

She sought Ben's gaze and nodded at him. "Good morning."

"Hey," he nodded back.

"This young man is here for fishing gear." Hazel moved to the wall displaying rods. "Wants to try his hand at an island pastime." She removed one to inspect it, but her attention bounced between them.

"Oh, right." She relaxed and leaned against the counter. "We can outfit you with whatever you need. What kind of fish do you want to catch?"

"Big ones!" Hazel chuckled and wiggled her eyebrows.

"Start at the top. Aim for the stars. Conceive, believe, achieve, right?" Ben laughed along with Hazel, encouraging a laugh from Ginny too.

"You're a positive person, young man. I like that." Hazel's eyes flashed as she handed a rod to Ben. "I just had a fantastic idea."

Ginny's heart fluttered. Hazel's ideas seldom worked in her favor.

~

A FEW HOURS LATER, Ben let fly another cast off the Avon Pier, fatigue tugging at his forearms.

"Nice one. Did you see the arc? You're getting really good." Ginny's praise boosted his flagging enthusiasm.

He reeled in the line as his stomach growled. Hoping the wind swallowed up the sound, he angled away from her.

"I guess the Apple Ugly's gone, huh?" She grinned.

"Well, we've been out here most of the morning. That Death by Sugar blob you shared is history." He reeled in the lure, the tug in his biceps reminding him to upgrade his upper body workouts.

She cast her line into the rolling water several feet farther than his had reached. "Hazel must have a crush on you. She never relinquishes her portion of our Apply Ugly. In fact, she sometimes cuts the halves more toward the third, two-thirds portions. She loves those things."

"Another fan right here. Tell me again what time I have to get to the Apple Blossom Cafe to buy some."

"Orange Blossom. During shoulder or off season, at least by mid-morning. Depends on how many visitors are on the island really. During the summer, good luck getting one. Once the day's offering is gone, you're out of luck."

"Like the fish, apparently." He flicked his wrist mimicking Ginny's cast and plopped the sinker a decent distance from the pier.

"Nice. That's your longest cast right there." She turned back to him. "Fishing is all about patience. Some days the fish are biting. Some days, not so much. Today's a not-so-much day. Next time, you can start earlier. You won't have to buy all this sweet new equipment." She laughed. "You had some good casts, though, and you caught a fish. Don't forget your fish."

"Right. The tiny fish clearly didn't know better than to bump up against my hook."

"When Hazel asks, say you caught a fish. She doesn't have to have details. Less is more."

"Got it." He nodded. "To hear her tell it, you're an A-number-one fisherman, ah, fisherwoman?" He chuckled. "But you didn't really fish today, just casted and reeled in to show me the ropes. Didn't want to make me look bad, huh?"

Sand-colored tendrils of hair danced around her up-tilted face.

"You held your own very well, and you didn't hook yourself. Good job." She smoothed a wind-battered wisp behind her ear. "Take everything Hazel says with a grain of salt. Maybe a bag of salt sometimes."

His stomach growled again, disrupting his attention on her tresses.

Ginny captured his glance with sparkling eyes, and air caught in his lungs. She pressed her lips together.

"Go ahead. Laugh. I can take it."

"Why don't we call it a day, so you can quiet your rumbling stomach?" She leaned her pole against the railing.

After the requisite new employee lunch with his coworkers at the branch, he'd eaten every meal solo all week. Conversation with an interesting and lovely companion, however, enticed him more than a double cheeseburger with a side of fries.

"Sounds great. Where should we go?" He grabbed his rod and reel in one hand and his tacklebox with the other.

She slid the strap of the empty, brand new soft cooler onto her shoulder.

"My treat. For teaching me how to fish." Come on. Say, yes. Let's keep this day going a little longer.

"Well, I have—"

"To eat. Save me from another boring meal with this guy." He thumbed his chest. "Take me to a place only the locals know. Please?"

A tiny smile bloomed on her mouth. "Okay."

CHAPTER 4

*B*en slid in the door of the Kennekeet Community Church as members of the praise team took their places in front of microphones and instruments. Turning his phone back on this morning had revealed multiple family texts he'd respond to this afternoon and one interesting text from Ginny listing the worship service time. Not exactly an invitation but helpful information, perhaps, in developing this fledgling friendship.

Too bad he missed the early meet and greet time, but rolling out of bed twenty minutes till the service begins diminished the window of arriving early into a doggy door.

He scanned the sanctuary for a familiar head of dark blond hair. A movement near the arrangement of sunflowers caught his attention. Hazel. Hazel sitting behind the drum set. Behind the drum set? Holding a drumstick, she rubbed underneath her nose with an exaggerated movement.

Catching his eye, she turned her head toward her left. He looked toward his right and found her. Ginny sitting halfway up at the end of the pew. Instead of a braid today, she'd twisted her hair into a low knot on the side of her neck. Nice. He glanced back at Hazel and nodded his thanks. She smiled.

As he tiptoed up the side aisle, the worship leader signaled for the congregation to stand, and the beginning measures of a popular song floated through the sanctuary. Ben stopped at Ginny's pew and tapped her shoulder. The fleeting look of happy surprise on her face pinged through his chest.

"Sorry I'm late. Just saw your text a few minutes ago. Thanks for the invitation." He whispered.

"Glad you're here." Ginny shifted her gaze to the front, joining along with the singing.

After the last song, Hazel zigged and zagged, winding up right behind them in the aisle. "Welcome. Glad you made it."

"Me too." Ben stepped closer to Ginny to make room for Hazel and caught a whiff of some floral scent. Very glad.

"How was fishing?"

"Great. She's a good teacher."

"He's a fast learner."

"Wonderful." Delight animated Hazel's face. "You know, our first Christmas fishing tournament is in December. A great place to show your skills. And don't forget the gala planned to celebrate the winners."

"He might not be here then."

Ben started at Ginny's high-speed comment. True. A permanent replacement could happen any time, and he'd be back home, but still … He pushed the thought from his mind.

"Pshaw." Hazel's eyes lit up. "Hey, where're you two headed for lunch? Need a suggestion?"

"We ate lunch yesterday." Ginny lobbed a pointed glance to Hazel.

"You don't eat lunch every day?" She served one right back.

"Funny as ever, Hazel. I meant—"

Ben chimed in. "She means I hadn't asked her yet."

"Gotcha. So, where're you going?"

"She hasn't said yes either."

A faint pink tiptoed up Ginny's neck.

"Of course, she'll say yes, Virginia Rae. Why wouldn't she?" Exasperation punctuated Hazel's words.

"How about both of you joining me for lunch? My treat." Ben shifted his stance. "We went to Pete's yesterday, so—"

"You took him to Pete's?" Hazel's eyebrows doubled the space over her eyes. "Of all the places on the island." She shook her head.

"He wanted to go where the locals go." Ginny hugged her Bible in front of her.

"We had a great lunch."

"Yeah. Fish on wax paper. Standing at the bar."

"You can't beat delicious food, Hazel. It was delicious." Ben stepped an inch closer to Ginny.

"Wax paper and no ambiance. White walls all around except the Jesus wall. "

Ben chuckled. She had the decor down. The Jesus wall had a portrait of Jesus, Jesus Knocking on the Door, Jesus in Gethsemane, and several crosses for good measure.

"We ate at a picnic table. We could see the lighthouse, smell the ocean, hear the sea gulls. Plenty of ambiance."

"And the wax paper kept the fish tacos intact." He rubbed his hands together. "So, where're we going, ladies? I'm starving."

"Sorry. No can do. I got sweet potato biscuits and a bowl of fish chowder waiting for me." Hazel moved backward. "Thank you anyway. Take him to Calmside. They gotta view and fish on plates too."

"You up for it? Sounds good to me." Ben pushed his point, hoping to quell Ginny's hesitation.

"Sure. You can follow me. I'll wait at the first entrance." She pointed at the driveway on the south side of the parking lot.

"No. Better leave one car here and drive together. Then you

just need one parking place." Hazel focused her attention on Ben.

"She has a point."

Ginny sighed. "I know the way. I'll drive."

~

Why did Hazel play matchmaker to every male who crossed the shop's threshold? Poor Ben. He didn't know what he'd gotten into when he walked into the store last week. Ginny rotated the glass vase of yellow carnations and black-eyed Susans, considering ways to irritate Hazel. Not sharing an Apple Ugly this week. Having her start inventory early. Hmm. Not a bad idea.

Ben cleared his throat and made eye contact. "Hey, thanks for having lunch with me again. I'll thank Hazel too, for kinda elbowing you into it. I'm missing my weekly meal with my siblings, so ..."

Score a point for Hazel's insight. He'd been lonely all week and missed his sister and brothers. No wonder he'd visited the store twice in a row. A touch point from a long-ago memory, the store led him to two new friends on the island. His sudden appearance after two decades didn't mean anything and shouldn't stoke a schoolgirl crush.

Irritating Hazel might not be wise. She'd share the pastry, but the inventory idea ... "Happy to help." Enjoying some meals with him could work as long as she kept his temporary status in mind.

He leaned his forearms on the table. "So, Hazel's a drummer, eh? She sounded good up there with the praise band."

"She earned a music degree from Meredith College. If you're lucky, maybe you'll hear her sing sometime. She's got a beautiful voice. Music talent runs in that side of our family."

"You're related?"

"My dad's cousin. She moved back after retiring from

22

teaching music for decades in Chocowinity and helps out with the store now."

A waiter appeared and took their orders, leaving a basket of steaming hushpuppies.

Ben raised his eyebrows. "A Poke bowl? Is sushi an authentic Hatteras dish?" Grabbing a golden-brown nugget of fried cornmeal, he bit it in half.

She shook her head. "You can find it around the island now, but I discovered it in Raleigh when I lived there." She chose a small hushpuppy.

"College?"

"Grad school."

"Impressive. Business degree?"

"Linguistics." Her satisfaction enjoyed the surprise lighting his eyes.

"Didn't see that coming. What led you there?"

Her mind jumped back to the first day she'd seen them, three boys and a girl, eating ice cream in front of her dad's tackle shop. They jostled each other, teasing back and forth, oblivious to the little girl watching at the edge of the parking lot. Fascinated, she crept closer to eavesdrop. Hearing their desire to go crabbing, she jumped on a crazy plan before her courage disappeared like a sand bar at high tide.

"Wanna do us some crabbin'? Moy haise is right dain the road to the saind soid."

The four looked at her like she'd just spoken gibberish. Every *Ow* sound, the long *I* sounds had set her apart from the spellbinding, big city siblings.

"What did she say?" The youngest boy, the one they called Sam, asked.

But the sister, Josie, approached her, smiling. "You want to take us crabbing?"

And so began her week with the Daniels family. She'd spent time every day with them, showing off her part of the island. It

was also her first lesson in speech differences and how her Hoi
Toide language told stories way beyond her ten years.

"Hey, Ginny. Where'd you go?" Ben popped a second hush
puppy into his mouth.

She blinked. "Sorry. A memory highjacked me for a minute. I
wanted to study the Hoi Toide speech of the Outer Banks."

"Right. You don't sound like you have much of an accent
now."

Shrugging, she explained, "I lived off the island for a while."

"But the accent sounds so cool. Why would you want to
change?"

The waiter set dishes in front of them, saving her from
answering.

"Speaking of your dad ..." He unrolled his utensils.

"He passed away last fall. Would you like to try some of the
sushi?"

"I like my seafood with an internal temperature of cooked,
but thanks for offering. This clam chowder looks good." He
studied his bowl.

"New England and Manhattan have their offerings, but this
one, Hatteras clam chowder, is the best. No cream. No tomatoes.
Just sweet clam broth in all its goodness." She dug into her Poke
bowl, spearing a cube of salmon.

She still worked on her salad when Ben pushed his empty
bowl to the side of the table, snagging one last hushpuppy. "I
need some more practice fishing with a pro. You game?"

"I'm no pro—"

"You own a tackle shop. Don't sell yourself short. Help this
landlubber get better."

"Dingbatter." She threw out the island word and waited for
his reaction.

"What?"

"You're a dingbatter."

"Hey, now. I wasn't that bad. I caught a fish, remember?"

24

She chuckled and shook her head. "It means you're not from here. That's all." And here only for the interim, not forever. Remember that, Ginny. Still, pretending he lived here full-time—

"Hey, you know something else I'd love to try? Hang gliding." His eyes widened in excitement.

"You want to what?"

"Hang glide. It has to be crazy fun. Go with me. Give me pointers."

"I've never done it."

"You haven't? Then, for sure, we're going. I'm booking lessons. Maybe next weekend. The fish can wait."

CHAPTER 5

*B*en swiveled on the bench and leaned his back against the picnic tabletop in the green space behind the bank. A breeze from the sound ruffled the remnants of his takeout lunch. He grabbed his phone and found Ginny's thread. They'd taken to texting every other day or so. Nothing earth shattering, but he'd come to look forward to her humorous take on current events and instances from his workday and hers.

> Hey. Hang gliding is booked for this weekend and beyond. I'm on a wait list. How about another fishing lesson instead?

He tapped the family thread.

> If I can get us lessons, who's up for hang gliding Thanksgiving weekend?

He researched Hidden Hatteras Gems while he waited for responses. He hadn't read past the third suggestion when the first sounds buzzed his phone.

In like Flynn

Sam, of course. Always ready for anything.

Absolutely

Heath responded in the affirmative.

Hello? Thanksgiving. Three people from church are coming.

Josie. Planning ahead.

I'll try for the Saturday. Sound good?

About Thanksgiving.

Josie. Still hopeful for his appearance for the holiday.

It's a no go, sis. I'm working Friday. You travel here Friday. Hang
glide Saturday.

Another text buzzed through. Ginny. Nice.

Fishing works for Saturday. We need to start earlier.

When?

Sunup at the pier. I'll bring the bait.

Yes!

I'll bring the apple ugly and coffee.

Deal.

~

"GOOD AFTERNOON, MS. ..." Ben glanced at the folder on his desk.

"Burris. Yancy Burris."

He rounded his desk and gestured for her to sit in the chair opposite his. "Ms. Burris, how can I help you today?" He observed her work boots, faded jeans cuffed at the bottom, and faded barn coat.

Sharp, brown eyes narrowed when they caught him assessing her appearance. He smiled, hoping to disguise any unprofessional looks leaking out of his face.

"I need your services for an important matter, but we'll get to that later." She wiggled out of her coat and settled back into the chair.

An important matter? A loan, for sure. But for what? What would she need to buy now? If her crow's feet told the tale, she might be close to eighty years old. Her laser-like eyes, however, chronicled everything in the room. Her body movements indicated a spryness not always shared by her contemporaries.

Not so fast, Ms. Burris. This is still my office, temporary or not. "Right, ma'am. First National Bank provides several kinds of services to our clients. Loans—"

"I know what banks do." Jutting her chin forward, she emphasized each word with a tap on the chair arms. "I want to know about you. You're not from around here, are you?" Her face revealed she already knew the answer. She delivered a challenge, not a question.

"No, ma'am." Take charge of this conversation. He leaned toward her. "Are you here to apply for a loan, Ms. Burris?"

She blinked away his attempt at leading the chat. "We'll get to my business. Don't worry. Where're you from?"

"Charlotte."

"A long way from here." She stroked her chin. "So, you're taking over for Thumb Nelson."

He trapped a chuckle just before it escaped. Who is this woman? "Terrence Nelson?" He planted his elbows on the arms of the wingback chair and clasped his hands.

"Indeed. Some people call him Thumb. Unfortunately, he has no neck. His head juts out of his shoulders like a thumb."

"Right, ma'am. Ahm."

Her mouth twitched. "I'm glad you've got his job."

"Temporarily. Till a permanent manager is hired."

"Neither here nor there." She flicked her hand to delete his words. "I'm just glad they got rid of Thumb. Finally."

"Terrance Nelson retired." *Engaging in gossip is never a good look, Ben. Redirect the conversation. Put the kibosh on these rumors.*

"So you say, but I know what the scuttlebutt is. His vices finally caught up with him, the Namby Pamby."

"Ms. Burris—"

"Call me Yancy if we're going to be working together." She narrowed her eyes. "My plain talk shocks your sensibilities, but I never cared for Thumb. Unfortunately, my money was already here when he got the job.

"Mr. Nelson—"

"Was a Namby Pamby."

"You've said. Now about your business—"

She cocked her head. "How do you find surfing?"

"I'm sorry. What?" This woman had clearly fallen off her rocker. Surely someone would be searching to return her to the rest home she must have escaped from this morning.

"Surfing. You know, waxed boards."

"Yes, ma'am. I've tried it a few times. Never got the hang of it. Not too many gnarly waves where I come from." He grinned over his clasped hands.

She captured his gaze with a severe, brown-eyed stare

successful in melting his grin. "You think you know some of the language though, don't you, young man?" She raised an eyebrow. "I've never cared for silly new words myself. Silly old words like my favorite, pixilated? That's a different story."

Heat rolled inside his chest and crawled up his neck. He shifted in the leather chair, hoping to distract from his discomfort. This old woman had teacher eyes. "Are you talking computer graphics?" A relatively new word, for sure.

"No, sir. I am not talking about computer graphics. I believe you're confusing synonyms. Look it up." She folded her arms. "So, you're not a surfer. Disappointing, but not a deal breaker. Get that Stowe girl to take you some time."

Ben's mouth dropped open. He snapped it closed.

"Scuttlebutt. Plus, I've seen you together here and there with my own eyes. You couldn't do better than Virginia Rae. Her family goes back a ways here on the island. You'll find some Stowes buried up in the cemetery in Old Hatteras Village." She nodded. "Surfing. Try it before you go back inland." She stood, slipping on her coat before he could offer assistance.

He popped to his feet to keep up with her.

"Thank you for your time today." She halted, turning at the door and smiled, her first one of the meeting. "I'll be seeing you again, young man."

"Yes, ma'am." He sagged against his closed door.

Yancy Burris, a character, for sure. Glancing at his watch, he chuckled to himself. Another island character, Hazel, expected him bright and early in the morning for help with a Christmas project.

Taking down decorations from her attic? Putting up lights?

Whatever the job, it didn't matter. Ginny would be there too.

Hatteras, your women fascinate me. What other attractions do you have?

CHAPTER 6

ollowing Hazel's instructions, Ben poured two cups each of Brazil nuts, English walnuts, and pecans into the stainless-steel bowl. "That's a lot of nuts."

"Now, take this chopper and start chopping, not to nut dust, but just break them up. Makes for easier slicing." Hazel checked on Ginny's pot with the condensed milk and bag of marshmallows. "Is the eye on low? Don't turn it up high. Melt them slow and easy so you don't burn the bottom."

"Yes ma'am. Will do." Ginny stirred and sent a quick smirk to Ben.

"I'm teaching you the right way to make these fruitcakes, Miss Priss. Cook it low and slow so you don't—"

"Burn it. Got it." Ginny dragged the oversized spoon through the milky, gooey mixture.

"With all these nuts, shouldn't we call them nut cakes instead of fruitcakes?" Ben raked the chopper through the bowl, redistributing the whole nuts with the chopped ones.

Hazel greased another mini loaf pan. "The fruit comes from the raisins, dried figs, and maraschino cherries."

"Are those cherries really fruit, though?"

"Quit giving me a hard time. Chop, Ben."

"I'm chopping. I'm chopping. Let's think about a name change. Fruitcakes have such a woeful reputation. Nut cakes, now, they sound—"

"Nut cakes sound better than fruitcakes? Really?" Hazel turned up the volume on her CD player. Bing Crosby silky voice filled the kitchen. "I love 'Christmas in Killarney.'"

"Maybe fruitcakes need new PR." Ginny arched her eyebrows, a teasing set to her mouth.

Ben caught Ginny's glance behind Hazel's back and held it. The blush creeping into her cheeks raised the hair on the back of his neck.

"Christmas music already?" He focused on Bing instead of Ginny.

"Sets the mood, and you people like to talk. We need to work. You know you didn't have to help."

Ginny dropped her gaze to the pot. "Right. You guilted me into helping. You held your health, or rather, the ruination of your health over my head. No whining from you next week."

"If I'd had to chop nuts for three batches and stir all this gooey stuff together by myself, my arm and back would've been out of commission for more than a week. You're getting a great end of the deal. Sparkling company on a Saturday morning and a fruitcake to boot. Plus, I don't have to call in sick."

"Sometimes I think I—"

"Hey, ladies. Are these nuts okay?"

Hazel peered into the silver bowl. "Looks good. Now add the raisins. Golden and regular. Both boxes."

"Gotcha." Ben opened the red box and shook the clump of dark raisins into the nuts.

"Add the golden ones and stir. Then you'll be ready for the graham cracker crumbs." Hazel inched toward Ginny.

"I'm still stirring."

"Don't let it burn." Hazel checked the control knob and lowered the flame a touch. "Low and slow."

"If you say that one more time—"

"Ladies, let's keep our eyes on the prize." Ben smiled to himself. These two bickered like siblings. A pang squeezed his heart for the three he left in Charlotte.

GINNY PRESSED HER LIPS TOGETHER. Hazel had a knack for grating all over her nerves. And in front of Ben too. He probably thought their squabbling childish. Note to self: *Focus on the pot and the sweetly scented steam rising from the concoction. Stir from the bottom so the milk wouldn't burn.* She'd never hear the end of it if the milk burned.

Hazel was trying her hardest to matchmake the two of them. Why did she like Ben so much? Granted, he was good-looking, smart, kind, interested in island history, folklore, and events. She smiled to herself. He sounded like the full package. Except for one enormous hurdle. His life existed seven hours away near his tight-knit family who clamored for him to come home.

Excursions to fish, to eat together, and to make fruitcakes were fine and good, but she'd keep her head on straight ... and forget about the look they just shared.

"Hey. Ginny. Look out." Hazel bumped her away from the stove with a hip and grabbed the spoon. "Were you asleep, girl?"

"I was stirring."

"You were daydreaming. Oh, the fruitcake woman never had as much trouble as this."

"The fruitcake woman? A neighbor?" Ben dutifully stirred his bowl, pulling the nuts, raisins, and figs up from the bottom to the top of the pile and going back down for more.

"No. She's in a Truman Capote story." Hazel shook the box of graham cracker crumbs into the bowl of nuts and dried fruit.

"Yeah. I remember it. What's it called?"

"'A Christmas Memory.'" Ginny circled her spoon all the way around the pan and then down through the middle casting her mind to the sweet story of a little boy and his aunt.

"That's it. A professor read it in class one day during a freak snowstorm. Just a handful of us attended class. She got choked up reading it, and Christmas was past. Already January."

"People here celebrate Christmas in January too. Old Christmas. Ever heard of it? Nothing wrong with Christmas in January."

Ginny held her breath and began counting. One Mississippi. Two Mississippi. Three—

"In fact," Hazel paused, checking the stove knob again.

Here it comes.

"If you're still here in January, you can celebrate Old Christmas. Right, Ginny? Ride up to Rodanthe for the party. Maybe Big Buck will show up."

Stop coming up with outings, Hazel.

"January is a long way away. I'm sure the bank will have a new manager by then." Remember, Ginny. He's leaving.

"Trying to get rid of me?" Ben grinned. "We've had some résumés come in, but I'm not involved in the process. Big Buck, huh?"

"Two men dressed up like a shipwrecked cow that wound up here years ago." Ginny pointed to her pot. "This looks ready, Hazel. All the marshmallows are melted."

Hazel nodded. She dumped chopped cherries into the bowl of nuts. "Now pour the bottle of cherry juice into your pot, Ginny, and keep stirring."

The juice tinted the milky mixture with a faint pink.

"Okay. Be careful now and pour your pot over Ben's bowl. Easy. Don't splash it. You'll burn your hands but good." Hazel kept careful attention on the process. "Yes, now stir it all together. Ben, you got strong arms. Put 'em to good use."

Ben chuckled. Ginny turned to the sink to rinse out her pan and keep her eyes off Ben's strong arms.

"Once all that's mixed up, we fill these little tin loaf pans and start all over again."

THREE HOURS LATER, Ben's strong arms ached as he navigated Highway 12 for the beach access. A run on the beach would get the kinks out.

Those cakes better be delicious. They were a bear to make. All that chopping and stirring, but Ginny was a trooper. She followed every one of Hazel's directions with just a couple of quirked eyebrows.

Turning off the highway, he coasted to a stop in the sandy lot. He jogged over the path leading to the beach and kicked off his New Balances. Digging his toes into the wet sand, he dipped his fingertips into the surf, a new take on his warm-up stretches. He checked his watch and aimed for the lighthouse.

Forty minutes later, he splashed through the surf to cool down and headed for his car.

He grabbed a towel from the back seat, wiped his face and hands, and picked up his phone. Ten messages from his siblings and one from Ginny. He read hers first.

Thanks for helping with the fruit cakes. You made Hazel's day.

She sent it an hour earlier. He checked his watch again. Almost four o'clock.

Make mine. Have dinner with me.

He sent the text and checked the ones from his family. Lots of chatter about Thanksgiving. No holiday at home for him. As the newest person in the office, and a temporary hire at that, he'd missed the time to request off the Friday after Thanksgiving. Only one person, Felicia Combs, would be off that day to enjoy her home-from-college children. His phone signaled a new message.

Sounds good. Did you fish this afternoon?

No. You're my fishing buddy. Ran instead. Let's go out.

GINNY READ THE TEXT. Her heart fluttered. Fishing buddy. Calm down, heart. Fishing buddy equals buddy. Which is fine. Nothing's wrong with being a buddy. Helping Ben out. Having dinner with him to keep him from eating alone. She texted back before she could rain all over the fun prospect of being with Ben a second time in one day.

Sure. Where? What time?

Calmside? We can watch the sunset, right? 6:00? Text me your address.

Her heart flipped again. He'd pick her up? Was this a date or a don't-let-me-be-lonely dinner? What would she wear?

Sounds good.

She also texted her address and camped out in front of her closet going back and forth between casually chic and island dressy.

An hour later she slipped into the casually chic outfit she hadn't worn since Raleigh. It had languished in the back of her closet waiting for the perfect outing.

Please, Lord. Let this be a perfect night.

CHAPTER 7

*B*en held the chair for Ginny. "Will your jacket be enough out here? I've got a sweatshirt in the car. Or we can get a table inside."

"I'm good. November evenings haven't turned too cold here yet. We want to see the sunset, right?" She nodded out over the calm water.

"Yeah. The view's great. So's the food."

"Some say the best on the island."

"You don't? The chowder was excellent."

"The food's delicious, but you'll find the best cooks at the church's potlucks."

"Gotcha. When's the next potluck?" He smiled at her.

And she wished for one on the calendar. "I'll let you know."

Their conversation, easy and fun and interesting, moved from one topic to another without falling into rough places or rocky patches, chasing one rabbit trail after another until dessert time. Ben scanned the menu. "Are you up for something sweet?"

"Always."

"Ah, a sweet tooth, eh?"

"Order the fig cake. It's an island thing."

"Figs? Again? Hazel promised us our own fruitcake, and you want to order one?"

"It isn't a fruitcake. It's a fig cake, and it's delicious. You have to try it before you leave." Yes, keep thinking about when he leaves. As fun as it is to chat over dinner, he will leave and go home. All the way to Charlotte.

"Is that okay?" Ben and the waitress waited for her to answer.

At her blank look, the waitress rescued her. "The slice is pretty big. You probably want to share."

She nodded. Sharing dessert. Hoo, boy.

~

"I ADMIT. This fig cake is pretty good." Ben stuffed another forkful into his mouth.

"Pretty good? Tell you what. You need to try one of Yancy Buriss's. She's the best."

"I've met her. She wants me to learn to surf."

"Oh, yeah?" Ginny laughed. "Is she going to teach you?"

"She said *you* should take me."

"She's the expert."

He sipped his coffee. "She surfed?"

"As far as I know, still does. I saw her on the waves twice last summer. She swims in the ocean almost every day. If the current's too strong, she'll swim in the sound. If you mention swimming pools in front of her, she'll call you a Namby Pamby."

"Right. She used that term in my office."

Ginny chuckled. "Probably about Terrence Nelson."

Ben glanced at her.

"Yep. I'm right. No love lost there. Not since he bowed out of a charity surfing tournament."

39

"Didn't donate money to the cause?" This isn't gossip, right? It's getting to know my clients, right?

"He didn't surf. She wanted to beat him."

Ben chuckled. "Sounds about right from the little I know about her. She thinks a lot of you." He drained his coffee cup, jolted by an impulse to smooth a wisp of hair behind her ear.

Shoving that reaction out of his mind, he broached a safer topic. "Hey, where's a good place for local gifts? I thought I'd treat my family to beach Christmas presents this year."

DARKNESS COCOONED them on the drive down Highway 12. Ben adjusted the radio to a local station playing piano music. He glanced at Ginny. "Are you warm enough?"

She nodded. "I enjoyed hearing about your siblings. And Josie's getting married next summer?"

"Yeah. To a great guy. We weren't exactly sure at first, but he's a keeper. He holds his own with all our smack talk."

"Sounds like a fun time when you're together."

"For sure. I'll miss them at Thanksgiving." Having planted the seed, Ben focused on maneuvering her driveway, waiting.

"You'll be here for Thanksgiving?"

"Uh-huh. I work Wednesday and Friday. One day off isn't really enough time to go home." He switched off the ignition and set the parking brake. Was that enough information to get her mind going? Would he have to straight up ask for an invitation? "I'll walk you up."

He met her at the front of his crossover, chanced a quick glance in her direction. Her eyes scoured the ground. Was she considering asking him?

"Ahm. Hazel's having people over, including me. For Thanksgiving, I mean."

Bingo.

"I'm sure she'd love to have you too. I'll mention it to her."

"Well, I don't want to intrude." But he really did. A turkey sandwich in his room at the bed and breakfast verses a real meal? With Ginny? No contest.

"If she found out you spent Thanksgiving alone, I'd never get back on her good side." She continued toward her front porch. "You'll have the invite ASAP."

"I look forward—"

"Hey, Ginny." A disembodied voice carried from somewhere on the porch.

She gasped and made a hard stop. Ben knocked into her back.

"Tad?" Ginny's voice held surprise and some other emotion.

"The one and only." A smile colored the statement. A friendly smile or a menacing one?

She turned to Ben. "I'm sorry. Thank you for dinner. Ahm." She glanced to the porch.

A movement and the rocking chair, freed from a weight, rocked back and forth. "Don't let me break up your evening. I was just enjoying the night air."

"I'll tell Hazel, and … and see you, okay?" She held up a flattened hand as if to ward him off.

Why didn't she want him to meet this person?

"Is everything good?" He lowered his voice to a whisper. "Are you okay? Do you want me—"

"Yes, I'm fine. Thank you for dinner." She nodded and headed for the porch steps. "Tad, why are you here?"

Ben hesitated. Ginny sounded more like herself after the momentary shock of finding someone rocking on her front porch. He watched as she unlocked the front door and let the man inside.

God, what to do here?

WRUNG OUT FROM THE NIGHT, Ginny leaned against her bedroom door. The evening had begun so nicely with Ben picking her up, chatting over the delicious meal, watching the sunset, and sharing the fig cake. Perfect really until ...

Tad.

Why did he have to show up now?

Tad.

Her phone buzzed. She looked at the notifications. A text from Tad and two from Ben.

The first from Ben, a half hour ago.

Just checking in. Everything good?

The new text read,

Calmside was great. So was the company. Even the fig cake.

She tapped the message bar.

Thanks for checking in. I'm fine. Told you the fig cake was good.

Then opened Tad's.

Didn't mean to surprise you. Don't be mad.

A new text came through. From Ben.

Sorry. My older brother status is shining through.

You're a good brother. Good night.

Sighing, she headed toward her bathroom to pluck out her

contacts. Tad had told her the beginning, but there'd be more. She swapped her tunic and tights for a hoodie and sweatpants. Might as well be comfy. Knowing Tad, the story would take a while to tell. A long night stretched in front of her.

She opened her door to the smell of coffee. A long night indeed.

CHAPTER 8

*B*en grabbed the back of the pew in front of him to keep his fingers from drumming during the benediction. Why hadn't Ginny shown at church? He hadn't texted since the good night text last night, but his fingers itched to send How are you? or at least Good morning. Would he be overstepping, hovering like Josie always accused him of doing?

Dial back the concerned older brother routine. You already played that card last night.

He waited for Hazel near the cornucopia in the vestibule. "Good music this morning."

"Thanks. I try. Where's our girl?"

"I was hoping you'd know."

"Haven't heard from her since the fruitcakes yesterday."

"When I dropped her off last night, someone was on her front porch."

Hazel's eyes lighted. "Dropped off as in after a date? Where'd you go?"

"Not important right now, but we ate at Calmside. Do you know Tad?"

"Tad's back?" Hazel's eyes narrowed, extinguishing the light of a second ago.

"Who's Tad?"

Hazel made a face. "Oh, boy. And I'm on the church steps."

"You don't have to say anything you'll regret. Is it the guy who broke her heart in Raleigh?"

She sighed and shook her head. "He's her ... wayward brother."

Brother, huh? His shoulders released a bit of tension. "Wayward?"

She pulled him away from the diminishing crowd. "Tad's had a rough go of it for the past few years. Since he was a teenager really. Most of his own making."

"Gotcha."

"Didn't know he was back in town."

"He surprised Ginny too."

"Last night. Dang it. I want to hear all about your supper, but I need to get over to Ginny's. Check things out."

He tensed again. "Is she in danger?"

"Oh, no. Tad loves his little sister. It's himself he has a problem with. I'll drop by, ask her why she didn't come to church. You know. Be my nosy self." She gazed over the glistening sound and shook her head again. "Did you have the fig cake? Tell me that at least."

"Yep, and it was delicious."

～

GINNY TIPPED her coffee cup to her mouth. Empty. The time on her phone screen nudged her to lunch, but she made no move to leave her chair on the back porch. She woke up an hour ago, too late for church. She switched on a favorite praise channel, hoping the music would lift her out of the funk stoked by her brother's appearance last night.

Tad. Why did you choose last night to come home? She released an extended sigh.

Thank You, God, for getting Ben away before Tad could … be Tad in front of him.

How to explain Tad to Ben? Maybe she wouldn't have to. The checking in texts were comforting, but they'd made no mention of a next time. Would they have a next time?

"You hoo. You back here?" Hazel rounded the corner.

Ginny leaned her head on the back of her chair. "He's still asleep."

"Sleeping it off, huh?"

"No. Not this time."

"How much does he need?" Hazel dropped into the rocking chair beside her.

"He's got a job."

Hazel raised her eyebrows and rocked in silence.

"At a tackle shop up near Nags Head. For six months. In fact, he just got promoted to manager in September." She quashed the feather-light hope that wanted to settle in her heart. It was too early to contemplate her return to Raleigh.

"The college kids went back to school, eh?"

"Hazel."

"That boy." She tut-tutted and searched the horizon. "So much potential."

"Says he's been sober since Dad's funeral. He had a job in Hillsborough but wanted to get to the coast. He has a couple of days off."

"So, he just shows up out of the blue. Blindsides you instead of calling, not even texting you a heads-up first."

"Wasn't sure I'd talk to him. He came to apologize." Ginny swiped her thumb over the shell imprint in her mug.

"You've never not talked to him."

"The last time we talked I yelled at him. I … it was bad." She shuddered at the words in her mind she couldn't erase.

"You're expecting me to fail."

"I don't expect the people around me to fail. You just keep doing it. I expect the people around me to succeed. You've never stuck with anything long enough to succeed."

She'd show him more grace this time. *Please help me show him more grace this time.*

"Don't beat yourself up. He made his own bed. And now I guess he needs a ride back up the coast, or has he already lost his job?"

"Hazel, listen to me. We stayed up till 4:30. We yelled. We cried. We laughed some too. I've never seen him like this. He seems for real."

"Well, I hope to heaven it is, but he's gone sober before and fallen off the wagon more times than a shark's got teeth."

"He didn't ask for anything. I didn't promise anything. I just listened." But if he did stay sober ... Raleigh is a lot closer to Charlotte—stop. She pressed the back of her head into the wooden slats of the rocking chair. Don't count your pearls before you open the oysters.

"I hope you're right. For his sake and ours."

They rocked in silence and listened to the seagulls. Ginny counted three wind surfers on the sound.

"So, I heard you turned someone else on to fig cake."

"Hazel." She shook her head. "Leave it alone. He didn't want to eat another meal by himself."

"You could have ordered pizza at Gidgette's. You went to Calmside.

"He wanted to eat and watch the sunset."

"He's a romantic."

"He's leaving when the bank hires a new manager."

"Quit raining on my parade." Hazel rocked harder. "Let an old girl have some fun."

"You could have a lot of fun if you'd pay Red Basnight any attention."

Hazel fluttered her hand. "Pshaw. You don't know what you're talking about."

"Neither do you." Ginny grabbed her coffee mug. "Did you ask Red to Thanksgiving? Ben needs an invitation too."

"Wonderful. I'll see to it."

CHAPTER 9

"*C*orrect me if I'm wrong, but I think we just hiked through the Sahara Desert." Ben's baby brother, Sam, had a point.

The Jockey's Ridge State Park sand dunes, famous as the largest natural living sand dune system, dwarfed those nearer the seashore. Ginny had forgotten their stark, desert-like beauty in the fifteen years since she'd last been here for a youth group picnic.

Other groups had begun ascending the largest dune, heading toward the hang-gliding kites perched on top. She tamped down rising panic as she envisioned herself hanging from one of those kites and barreling toward the earth, screaming for help.

"And that looks like a mighty high hill we gotta climb." Sam's yellow helmet swung from his arm as he trudged over the sandy path. "You know, Ben, this jaunt sounded like fun before we had to get up at half past the crack of dawn just to get here."

"Sand dune, bro. If you're going to complain all day, go take a nap in the car. I'll take your flights." Ben bopped Sam on the head with his water bottle.

"Cut it out. I'm here and staying. Gotta show you how it's done."

The whole group laughed at Sam's bravado. Ginny hoped she'd be laughing at the end of this outing. Why didn't she bow out, opt for a morning on the water instead? She wanted to experience Ben's siblings again, that's why. Exactly the same, except twenty years older, they jostled each other, teasing back and forth in a choreography practiced for decades.

Right. A fun day except for the part about jumping off the side of a cliff strapped to a kite. Okay. Not a cliff. A really tall sand dune. With solid ground to hit after a fall.

"I'm still so full of turkey, I don't know how the kite will lift me off the ground." Ches tugged on his vest.

"Yeah, I noticed how shy you were digging into the turkey sandwiches yesterday. Not. Did you eat three or five?" Heath, the middle brother, chimed in.

"What can I say? Your sister's a great cook." He cupped Josie's elbow as they started the climb to the top.

"Thank you." Josie smiled and blew him a kiss.

Ginny mentally reviewed the steps from the mandatory lesson after all the consent forms were signed. So many steps to follow. How could she remember them all, not look stupid, and have fun all at the same time?

"Are you okay?" Ben's concern chipped away at her apprehension.

Pretending could lead to reality. Maybe. "Sure. It's all good." She wiped a trembling hand over a sweat-dotted upper lip.

"I can hear you breathing, and you're not out of shape." He grabbed her fingers. "Your hand is freezing."

"Kinda chilly today, don't you think?"

"Ginny, it's at least sixty-five degrees. Windy, yes, but the sun's warm." He dropped his voice lower. "You're okay with this, aren't you? It'll be fun."

"Heights aren't really my thing." She kept her eyes on the

ground, ignoring her peripheral vision where waves broke on the ocean side of the island.

They crested the dune and took their places near Josie and Ches.

"We're not going up too high. We're just flying off the dune and landing in the sand down there." He pointed to the path they'd just traversed.

"Did you hear what you just said? 'Flying off the dune.'"

"Sailing then. Is that better?"

"If we were talking water, yes."

He chuckled. "It'll be fun. I promise."

"Don't promise—"

"Huddle up, folks." Brody, one of the instructors, directed everyone to group together according to the name on the yellow slip of paper he'd given them back at the rental shop. Groups formed based on weight.

Josie and Ginny were grouped with a dad and two teen-aged daughters. Ches and the brothers comprised another group. Three more groups made up the whole class.

"Remember each of you gets five flights. Everyone flies once, and we then start over. Okay, where's Brody's group?" The instructor called Eli moved over to a group of twenty-somethings sporting college sweatshirts and Vans.

He stepped toward Ginny's group. "All right. Who wants to fly first?"

Ginny's stomach clenched, and she stepped back.

"Me." One of the sisters hopped forward.

"Cool. Remember you're going to rest your hands on the crossbar like this." He held out his arms, curving his hands over a pretend bar. "Then bend your chest over a little bit. Remember the pterodactyl pose, right?"

He held up the kite as the youngest sister disappeared under it. The group to the left of them already had a person in the air, sailing down to the valley below. A peaceful sight, floating in the air, the kite landing gracefully like an autumn leaf.

Ginny glanced over at Ben's group. Ches, clipped to his kite, walked, then jogged, then ran, and then he floated in the air to the encouraging shouts from his future brothers-in-law. Holding a leader rope, his instructor ran beside him down the dune. Ches soared all the way into the sea oats on the other side of the path.

"Woo-hoo. He's a natural." Sam cheered the loudest.

"He's my guy." Josie chuckled and gave him a thumb's up.

Everyone was laughing and clapping and having an all-around great time. Ginny secured the last spot for a turn. While both waited their turn, Ben stepped over beside her.

"How's it going over here?" He smiled, his face full of hope.

"You must be excited. I can't believe you got openings this weekend."

"I kept calling for cancellations. The guy took pity on me and pulled in another instructor. Pays to be persistent." He trapped her gaze. "And I am." He pulled on the straps of his vest. "Hey, sorry they still didn't have room for Tad.

"No worries. He had to go back up to Nags Head."

"I enjoyed talking with him on Thanksgiving."

She nodded. "It was a good day." She smiled. "Thanks again for the flowers. Hazel got a kick out of them. I liked mine too."

"Glad to hear it." He motioned to the other groups. "So, you've had a chance to study all these beginners. Got a game plan?"

"Giving my turn to that eight-year-old in the next group who could be the star of his own hang-gliding show sounds like a plan. Josie's pretty much a pro already too."

"Generous gesture but no fun for you. It'll be great. Just relax."

"All right. Ready for the last one in our first round. Come on up." Eli motioned to Ginny. "Step over that bar and lie on your stomach. I'll clip you to the kite. Loosen up your shoulders.

Relax and have fun." He stepped to the side of the kite. "Okay. Stand up. Remember hunch over a bit. Pull in your elbows. No chicken wings." He laughed. "Chickens don't fly. We're aiming for the house with the three gables straight ahead. See it?"

Her stomach bottomed out. "All the way to the beach?"

"No. We're aiming for it. Now, rest your fingers on the bar and relax. Remember walk. Jog. Run when I tell you. Then push your arms straight forward. Got it?"

Ginny sucked in a breath. So much to remember. Relax the shoulders and keep the elbows in. Hold the bar lightly.

"Okay." Eli moved with her. "Walk. Walk. Jog. Jog. Run. Run. Run! Push out. Push out!"

Her feet bicycled in the air one moment, and the next she slid on her stomach in the sand. She wiggled her ankles. Nothing broken. Good.

"All right we won't count that one. Let's get back and try it again." He released her from the kite.

She'd floated all of four feet down an eighty-foot dune before belly flopping. And it didn't even count. She brushed the sand from her vest. Oh, joy.

BEN WINCED as Ginny's kite nosedived into the side of the dune. Again. He'd feel slightly better if she'd let him pay for today's lesson, but she'd refused. She refused to give up also. When the family of five bagged their last flights in search of a fast-food experience, their instructor had taken on Ginny as a pet project, pulling her out of Josie's group and giving her one-on-one instruction.

A good sport, she'd taken it in stride joking about remedial lessons with a private tutor.

Heath stepped beside him as they watched another attempt at flight. "Man, these instructors are ripped like Olympic athletes, running down the dunes then back up with the kites who knows how many times a day. No wonder their water bottles are gallon jugs." He shook his head. "She's determined, eh?"

"Stop staring at her. You're making her nervous." Josie took a swig of water. "Say a prayer instead, you goons. She's trying so hard."

"Maybe she needs to just relax and go with the flow." Sam stretched his arms over his head in a good morning yoga pose. Heath jabbed him in his side. "Oof. Cut it out, man."

"Eli told her to relax every time he hooked her to the kite. She's doing better with Hannah. Hey, look. There goes Ches." Josie grinned at her fiancé.

Ches sailed just as before but some difficulty wobbled the kite, bringing him down well short of his impressive first flight's mark. He managed to salvage it with a landing on his feet, however. Doing a happy dance, Josie cheered and waved.

If nosediving farther down the dune counted as improvement, then yes, Ginny was getting better. Incrementally, at least.

God, give her some success before the end, please.

Listening to her instructor, Ginny nodded and laughed. Ben's heart lightened.

Hannah stepped to the side and called out the commands. Catching air, Ginny's kite rose and floated down the dune.

"Yeah, baby," Brody watched from his kite.

But as quickly as she went up, she came down again before the bottom of the dune.

Oh, man. Her last try. Hannah disappeared underneath, and then Ginny crawled out from under the kite. She jumped up and down and gave a thumbs up sign.

The crowd at the top of the dune went wild with Josie leading the charge. "Good job. Way to go."

"That's it, folks. The last flight of the morning. Another group's coming in at one o'clock."

Ben retrieved Ginny's water bottle and met her at the bottom.

"Great job. You got the kite going. How'd it feel?'

She laughed. "For the ten seconds I floated, fantastic. I think I'll stick to watersports, though."

"There's still some sand on your Henley." Josie brushed it off. "At least you improved. My best flight was my first one. I belly flopped on my last one." Josie gave her a side hug. "I like your positive attitude."

The walk back to the rental office consisted of tallying up belly landings and feet landings and voting on who looked the goofiest in the helmets. More teasing occurred at the equipment return window.

Hannah approached Ginny with a folded slip of paper. "Sorry we couldn't let you try again. You were really getting the hang of it. Gotta get ready for the next crowd." She waved goodbye.

Ginny opened the note and laughed. "A twenty percent off coupon for my next adventure." She offered it to Ben. "Here you go."

"Not a chance. It's yours. Don't lose it. We'll try again."

That's a promise, Ginny.

CHAPTER 10

"*I*t's not far to the sound from here." Ginny shut the crossover's door and headed from the shop's back parking lot. They'd enjoyed quick, mid-week fish tacos at Pete's, and now the second part of the evening consisted of watching for shooting stars from the shop's dock. It extended farther out into the sound than hers and offered an unencumbered view. Hazel had insisted Ben couldn't miss the light show.

"There it is." Ben caught up with her.

"What?" She scanned the horizon.

"Your accent. Finally. It's back."

Her stomach tightened. She'd been so careful, talking like she still lived in Raleigh, but her comfort level rose every time they were together. One little *Ow* sound in one short sentence betrayed her. "Ugh. My dad paid a lot of money to universities for me to learn to talk without the Outer Banks brogue."

"Why would you want to? It's so cool."

She slid him an are-you-kidding glance.

"Ginny." His eyebrows bunched together. "What's up?"

"Come on. Let's get to the dock so we can see the stars better."

"Hey." He tugged the hood of her jacket as she glided past him, her posture rigid. "Something's going on. Why did you want to lose the brogue?"

Turning back to him, she stopped. He let go of the hood.

"It's not about losing it exactly. I know when and when not to use my Hatteras voice."

"I like the Hatteras speech."

She tsked. "You didn't used to."

"Huh? I don't remember you using it before tonight."

She pinned her eyes on him. "I'm not talking about now." Continuing onto the dock, she kept well in front of him. "Hazel'll be disappointed if we don't see any shooting stars."

"I'm not worried about the stars or Hazel's disappointment either. Let's talk. You're not telling me everything."

BEN STARED after Ginny's unyielding back as she left him for the end of the dock. What had just happened? His gut wrenched at her transformation from a light-hearted dinner companion to someone wounded and closed-off. What was going on in her mind? How could he get her to share her story? He wanted to know more about her, her hurts, and her dreams.

The rising anger at her pain surprised him. He wanted to protect her, help her. He caught up with her and clasped her hand. *Trust me, Ginny. I'll keep your story safe.*

At the end of the dock, she motioned to the beach towel he held with his other hand. "Spread it out to lie on or roll it up like a pillow.

He followed her lead to roll his towel.

She positioned her towel several inches from his. "We'll see some stars, but they'll be few and far between now. You'll have to be patient. The best time is supposed to be two in the morning. I plan to be asleep then."

"One of my strong suits is patience, Ginny. I'll be ready to listen when you're ready to talk."

Ben heard a flopping noise against the water near the right-hand corner of the dock.

"What was that?" He turned his head toward the blackness over the sound.

"Just a fish dancing on the water. You're fine. I won't let anything happen to you out here." She injected a light tone in her voice, probably hoping he'd forget about his questions.

"I remember all your skills—crabbing, shelling, driving a boat ..."

"Steering a boat, please."

"I can hear you laughing at me."

She quietened. "I don't laugh at people's differences."

"A loaded statement, for sure, Ginny."

No response.

"Talk to me." Ben broke the silence. "Please."

HER HEART POUNDED against her chest like waves during a nor'easter. Was she really going to have this conversation with him? After all this time, did it matter?

Why not tell him, Ginny? He's not the same as twenty years ago.

She'd redeemed the ten minutes that changed her life. Okay, God redeemed it. Used it for her good. Made her into the knowledgeable person of today. She had experiences and skills beyond the ones of her childhood.

The dark, a protective blanket, let her travel back to the defining scene without him watching her relive it. "The first time I saw all of you, you fascinated me. You laughed and scrambled together like a winning team after a playoff game. Even with the shoving and thumping heads and teasing, I could tell you loved each other. You enjoyed being around each other."

"We were crazy happy to be out of the car. We'd just spent all day in our minivan. Our parents let us walk up to the store so we wouldn't kill each other."

"I tried not to be jealous of Josie's pink shorts and sparkly top. I can still see the front of her shirt with a sequined strawberry in the middle. I wanted to be part of your group so bad." She blew out a long stream of air. "You talked about crabbing, and I offered to take you. The words were out of my mouth before I could think them.

"Your parents were gracious and invited me to dinner and to the lighthouse." She chuckled. "What a time I had with my fancy family from Charlotte."

"Fancy? You got us confused with another vacation family."

"Nope." She sighed. Why not spill all the beans? Isn't confession good for the soul or something like that? "And then, of course, I developed a little crush on the big brother."

"What?"

"Yep. My ten-year-old self thought you were all that and a bag of chips."

"And dip?"

She chuckled again. "Dip too."

Another fish slapped the water.

"Okay. That one was a lot closer and may be related to Moby Dick."

"We're fine." She reached over to pat his arm.

He captured her hand. "That week sounds like I remember it. Except for the crush part. So, what happened?"

"Look! There's one." Her free hand jerked toward the sky.

"Yes! I saw it. Cool." He jiggled her hand still in his.

"On your last day, I rode my bike to the path to your cottage. All of you were joking around, packing up the van. You said, 'Put it in the boot, Heath.' And Sam howled. He kept repeating, 'in the boot, in the boot.' Then all of you started saying words with our accent." He tightened his hold when she tried to wiggle free. "Vans don't even have trunks, but you made fun of the language."

Taking in a breath, she held it, willing her heart rate to slow. *I am not that little girl.* Ben is kind. It wasn't a big deal. *I just built it up to be.* Let. It. Go. She cleared her throat.

"I ... I heard all of you laughing. I realized the week was just a week to you, nothing special like for me. You'd let me tag along to listen to me talk and then you were trying to sound like it. And laughing."

"In the middle of the laughing, I hightailed it for home." She pushed out another breath. "I didn't want to stay and give you more words to mock."

He sat up and drew her with him to sit knee to knee, then clasped her hands. "Ginny, please believe me. We weren't laughing at you. Yes, we were being stupid, trying out different sounding words, but listen to me." He leaned closer. "We were not laughing at *you*."

She buckled under the intensity of his gaze, transferring hers to the moon beam shining on the water. Nudging her chin with one finger, he guided her face back to him, caressed her cheek with the back of his hand.

"We weren't. I promise you. All of us thought you were special. We were jealous of your girl-boss skills. We went to the store to say 'bye, but your dad said you'd gone to the beach."

"I know."

"He told you."

She shook her head. "I hid behind the counter, then went to the beach just to keep his honesty in tack."

"Do you believe me?" Ben's face inched closer to hers.

Strands of her hair swirled in the breeze reaching out to Ben, lighting on his jacket. "I want to."

He slid his hand beneath her braid, tugging her toward him

and brushed his lips to hers. "I w
second time with a firmness that p
cared about her as an adult and as
away, he held her gaze for a moment

She forgot about the hurt, about th
focusing, instead, on the heat rising ins.
was becoming more than a schoolgirl cru

CHAPTER 11

*T*he sunlight winked off the sound. Ben's office window served a tantalizing view of two sailboats enjoying a Monday morning water adventure. He swiveled in his chair, allowing his mind to skitter over the events of the long weekend, beginning with the surprised joy on Ginny's face at the bouquets of flowers he'd brought to Thanksgiving, one for her and one for Hazel, then the hang-gliding experience, the family's early send off yesterday, Ginny's revelations from last night. And, finally, the kiss.

He lingered on the kiss and smiled.

She seemed different after the kiss, not as reserved. Playful even. She'd explained how her hurt led to her interest in language and subsequent studies in communications and French. He chuckled, remembering his ridiculous attempt at a French accent. "*Parlez-vous français?*"

"That's all you know, right?"

"*Merci, rendezvous,* fondue, canoe—"

"Canoe?"

"Sounds French to me."

Her full-on laugh rewarded his whimsy, emboldening him to kiss her again.

Revealing conversations, shooting stars, and tantalizing kisses. Maybe the special night would signal a change in their relationship. A knock on his office door brought him back to the present. Right. Yancy Burris's meeting today. Felicia opened the door and ushered the older woman in.

Closing his door on the Christmas carol playing in the lobby, Ben offered one of the chairs in front of his desk to Miss Yancy, taking the opposite one for himself. Dressed again in the brogans and brick red barn coat, she looked more ready to milk cows or muck out horse stalls than discuss wealth management.

"It's good to see you again, Miss Yancy." Ben focused on the woman before him, pondering words to explain steps to establishing a scholarship. He'd checked her account after she booked this meeting. True, she had healthy holdings, but how strong would her account be if she encountered a long illness? Or if she lived for ten, fifteen more years?

"I'm happy to see you too." She considered him. "What's the difference between pixilated and pixelated?"

A grin broke across his face. "Pixilated with an *I* means crazy, confused, or wacky. Pixelated with an *e* means the individual pixels are visible in a computer graphic."

"Thank you for following through." She cleared her throat. "Now, as I told Felicia when I made this appointment, I need your help setting up scholarships and other things." She opened a satchel and extracted a manila envelope. "I've got my portfolio here for you to peruse."

At Ben's raised eyebrow, she continued. "You're familiar with my account here, right?"

"Yes, ma'am."

"Well, I have that much each in seven other banks in Dare, Pasquotank, Chowan, and Currituck counties, plus stocks and bonds."

Ben quickly multiplied seven times the amount he'd seen on her account balance this morning. He blanked his face as he'd perfected during board games with his siblings. Could what she said be true? Could she have liquid assets upward of half a million dollars. He swallowed.

She handed him the folder, eyes focused on him, and smiled. "Precisely. You're the perfect person for me. I don't like locals knowing about my business. You won't gossip because you don't know but two people, Hazel and Ginny. They're not gossipers either."

"How did you—" He slammed his mouth shut on his off-limits question. He wasn't used to a sum of money shocking words out of his mouth.

"Well. You are human after all." She laughed. "It's a valid question. I'm quite good at reading the stock market. And knowing when to buy and when to sell, of course."

Question almost asked and graciously answered. "But you don't know me from Adam. You're trusting me with your life savings?"

"I'm not as dumb as you think I look."

Ben opened his mouth.

"Stop. I know the impression I give. I also know the kind of person you are. I've done some digging. Your expertise is wealth management. I need my wealth managed."

"I'm the temporary manager for this branch."

"Yes, so we have to get the ball rolling, don't we? I've got the list of charities and how I want everything divvied up."

Ben read over the list. "Two scholarships at the high school?"

"Yes, one for the college-bound student. One for the skilled student. To encourage both. I've got the prompts for entry essays and requirements too."

She was thorough, he'd give her that. The high school, the public library, the turtle-saving group, the Keenekeet Church, the Hatteras lighthouse.

"You've got quite a list here."

"I've got quite a lot of money. I want to see it put to good use."

"Miss Yancy, you have all this worked out. You need a lawyer to make it official."

"Right. I have one."

"Then—"

"I'm consolidating my money. My lawyer tells me to choose one bank. Tells me it'd be best. I doubt that's true. I'm sure the bigwigs on Madison Avenue have money in more than one bank. I'm sure it'll be easier for him when he goes to drafting the letters and what not. But it's easier for me too, keeping up with all those bank statements."

She shrugged. "It's inevitable word will get out about my money now, but I've got it allocated along with the amounts. Nobody should come singing their sad songs to me. I don't want any hullabaloo either. We just have to finalize this and that."

"Yes, ma'am." He pinched the bridge of his nose.

"Got a headache, son?"

"No, ma'am." He shook his head. "Just didn't see this coming."

"How could you have?" She laughed again. "I want this tied up with a bow by my birthday, Old Christmas."

"Old Christmas."

"January sixth. You're too much of a gentleman to ask, so I'll satisfy your curiosity. I'll be eighty. You got about a month."

CHAPTER 12

"*W*ell, it looks like my first fish will be my best entry. No luck out there for me this morning." Ben had caught several in the waning hours of Hatteras's first Christmas Classic Fishing Tournament, but all were smaller than the one he caught on the first day of the contest. Ginny had continued to encourage him, but the fish weren't obliging.

"Your catch is respectable. Don't count yourself out." Hazel reached for the ringing phone behind the counter. "Stowe's Tackle." She listened, frowning. "Say that again." She harrumphed. "She's here now." She handed the phone to Ginny. "Tad."

"Hey." Ginny frowned. "I'm coming. Sit tight." She handed the phone back and glanced at Ben. "I need to go, but I'll see you at the gala, okay?"

"What's up, Ginny?"

"Tad needs help over on Shackleford Banks." Hazel pursed her lips. "Didn't exactly sound sharp, if you know what I mean."

Ginny made a face. "He needs me. I'm going."

"Need some help?" If the anxiety in her eyes rang true, she did—in a big way.

"Thanks. I'm good."

"Yes, she does." Hazel folded her arms together.

Ginny set her jaw. "No."

"Yes, girl." Hazel reached under the counter. "The sound's choppy today. You don't know what shape he's in. Thank you, Ben. She's stubborn."

The sound's choppy? Ben swallowed. Had he just volunteered to ride in a boat? *God, this won't be good.*

"I can be stubborn too." But could he ride in a boat with his dignity intact?

Hazel handed a key to Ginny. "Take the ski boat out back. It's got two life jackets. Take another one just in case." She pointed to one hanging by the back door. "Ben, we appreciate your help. Leave your wallet and anything you don't want to get wet here. I'll keep it safe."

Should he ask for Dramamine? He pushed his wallet and phone toward Hazel.

"Okay. Let's roll." Ginny's countenance matched the clouds swirling in from the ocean. No time for medicine, just a quick, *Help me out, please, Lord.*

A boat. On that choppy sound.

Shrugging on the extra life vest, Ginny stalked down the path toward the boathouse. She hopped onto the boat with ease. Ben hesitated on the dock watching the bobbing boat. Don't watch the boat. Look at her back.

His last boat ride, a humiliating fiasco with college buddies, was supposed to have been his last. He'd promised himself, but Ginny needed him. Tad's call shut her down, changed her from the encouraging fishing buddy to a silent, all-business woman bent on a mission. Her brother.

She pulled a vest from the dry well and tossed it to him. "Come on aboard." She grabbed the wheel and brought the engine to life.

Clutching the vest, he planted a foot on the boat's deck, the bobbing deck. His head swirled in time with his lurching stomach. He forced his other foot into place beside the first.

"Hang on." Ginny maneuvered the boat out of the slip.

The G-force pushed him against the seat. He closed his eyes. Bad idea. A warning seized his gut. He searched for a fixed point on the horizon. The horizon swayed. The clouds undulated. His brain see-sawed.

Breathe, Ben. You will help Ginny. You will not vomit in front of her.

God, help here, please.

Concentrate, man. He rested his clammy head on his forearm along the side of the boat. Think. Kissing Ginny the other night. Fishing this morning. Eating lunch.

Lunch. He lost it over the side.

Help her, Lord.

∽

A BREEZE BUFFETING her face over the windshield, Ginny urged the engine faster.

The phone call had changed Ben. He'd gone silent, watching the exchange with Hazel. What was he wondering? What would they find when they reached Tad? Had Ben ever dealt with someone who was high or drunk or not perfect like his siblings?

Tad had been fine on Thanksgiving for the hour he ate with them, but now … Would Ben get to see him in all his sullied glory? Would he thank God his siblings were fun and fully engaged as contributing-to-society adults?

It didn't matter what he thought anyway. He'd be back in Charlotte with his family soon.

Tad's slurred speech warned her what to expect when they found him. Hazel, why'd you have to drag Ben into the middle of Tad's mess? Tad, you promised you were for real this time. You said you weren't going back to your old life. You promised.

Ridiculous hopes of his taking the shop in her place evaporated like cotton-ball clouds before the rain. She growled, confident the motor's roar would smother it before reaching Ben's ears. She pointed the bow north and gave the engine full throttle.

The boat road a swell and slapped the water on the other side. She squeezed the wheel, planting her docksiders for balance. Cool, salty spray splashed over the bow of the boat, snatching her from the negative thoughts. She glanced back to check on Ben. Good. Still in his seat. The hard landing didn't bother him. Her attention back to the sound, she scanned the horizon and spotted the small island.

She glimpsed the Jon boat up near Craggy Point. Good, but where was Tad? Thank goodness he had enough sense not to drive himself back. Tad, why'd you have to come all the way out here to ... She spied him, leaning against the port side of the boat. Passed out?

Gliding the boat to shore, she dropped anchor. "Hey, Ben, could you—" Her request flew from her mind.

With hands clutching the side of the boat in a death grip, Ben's face was tinted green. He shifted then heaved over the side.

"Ben, you get seasick?" A coldness in her stomach matched the wind on her arms. "Why'd you come?"

He wiped his mouth on his shirt sleeve and groaned. "I wanted to help."

"Oh, man." She shook her head. *I'm in a fix here, God.* "Okay. Sit tight. I'll get Tad, and we'll be back to dry land before you know it." She jumped off the boat and splashed through the waves to shore. For the first time, she got a good look at Tad. He was white as the foam on the surf.

"Tad!" She plopped down in the sand beside him. The rag tied to his foot seeped with blood. She sucked in a lung full of air and held it with her eyes closed. Blood. Not good. She nudged his chin. "Tad, can you hear me?"

His eyes fluttered open and focused on her. "Hey. A shell ... Sorry."

"I thought ..."

Pain marred his face. "Sober."

Tears burned in the corners of her eyes. "Can you stand? You've got to get on the boat."

He mumbled.

She tugged on his arm, and another hand slipped under his other arm. "Ben, I told you to—"

Ben bent over and heaved again.

THE LAST OF Ben's dignity spilled onto the little island. He wiped his mouth on shirt sleeve again and avoided eye contact. "Ready to lift him?"

"Ben, you don't have to."

"On three. One. Two. Three." They lifted Tad to standing. He swayed, but Ben caught his shoulder. Leaning together, they waded into the surf. The boat rocked on the waves. Ben groaned at the sight and tasted bile.

Man, oh, man. *Please, God, need some strength here.* His head beat out a sick island rhythm.

By God's grace, they sloshed Tad to the boat. Ginny hopped over the side and lifted him as Ben pushed from underneath. Tad rolled over the side and slid onto the deck. Ben forced his fingers around the ladder and climbed onto the bobbing boat. Gritting his teeth at rising nausea, he focused on fresh drips of blood dotting the wood.

He ripped off his vest and long-sleeved T-shirt and unwound the saturated shirt on Tad's foot. He sucked air through clenched teeth at the freshly bleeding gash. A bright red spot quickly spread on his shirt he wrapped it over the wound.

The wind whipped up a massive crop of goose bumps. Ben slipped on his life vest.

Ginny blew on her fists, then worked to get a vest on her brother. She tried to latch the hooks but missed the closures three times in a row.

"Let me." Ben grabbed the hooks, determined to connect them even if his head exploded in the process. The closure fit together on the second try, but success offered little pleasure against the war in his body.

"Thanks. He's lost so much blood." She met his eyes for the first time. "If I go back to the shop ..."

"Go wherever he needs." He waved her on and dropped to the deck beside Tad.

She raised the anchor, fired up the motor, and turned the boat in the opposite direction, covering new territory on the choppier surf.

From his vantage point flat on his back, the gray sky threatened rough weather. *God. Help.*

~

AN ETERNITY LATER, Ben pushed to sitting as Ginny slipped the boat alongside the Avon Medical Office dock. She threw a rope toward the dock and cut the motor.

A male nurse waited with a wheelchair. Arms akimbo, Hazel shook her head, grim-faced. She bent to secure the rope.

"Well, you made it before the storm hit. Good girl."

Praise God for huge blessings like slowed storms, radios for calling reinforcements, and for Hazel's coming to the rescue.

Ben pulled on Tad's arm to help him sit up as the nurse hopped on board. Holding his breath as the boat rocked again, Ben prayed. *Don't let me throw up in front of this man.*

"Looks like you lost a ton of blood, buddy. Let's get you inside." Bracing one leg against the dry storage, the nurse gripped Tad and stood him in one move. "Hold him like this, ma'am, and I'll hop up. We'll get him on the dock and in the chair. No problem."

Clutching her brother, Ginny glanced at Ben. "Thank you. I couldn't have done it without you."

Her thanks, though well-meaning, missed the comforting mark. Retching scenes splayed prominently in his mind.

With the rope tied around a galvanized cleat on the dock, Hazel reached toward Ben to help him out of the boat. "Not a boat person, eh? No wonder you stick to pier fishing so much."

Ben grunted and let her steady him on the dock.

Satisfied with the safety of his patient, the nurse trekked to the building.

"I'll take it from here, Hazel. Thanks again, Ben. Go home and feel better." Ginny kept her hand on Tad's shoulder and skipped-walked to keep up with the wheelchair.

Gritting his teeth, Ben warned Hazel, "I'm not leaving yet." He set out after the group with the wheelchair. Hazel followed him, unusually silent.

Saving the last of his energy reserves, he rested his aching head against the wall in the Avon medical office. A miniature Christmas tree winked at him from the reception desk. With the pain hosting a party between his temples, he squinted at the swinging door to the examination rooms.

The male nurse emerged and offered him a scrub shirt with tiny Santa hats decorating it. "You might be more comfortable in this."

Comfortable had left the station a couple of hours ago, but a wet life vest or a dry scrub shirt? Even covered with Santa hats? No contest.

"Thanks, man." Ben popped the buckles and changed out of the vest. The soft cotton soothed his skin, cloaking him in a soapy smell.

The door swung open again. Ginny.

"I thought you two were leaving." She narrowed her eyes at Hazel. "He needs to go home."

"He wanted to check on you."

Her gaze flickered toward Ben. "I'm fine. Tad's getting stitched up right now. You need to get ready for the gala."

"I'm not worried about the gala." Ben shifted in his plastic seat, thought better about standing.

"You need to celebrate."

"Celebrating an honorable mention isn't important right now. Being here with you is important now."

Tears sparkled in her eyes. She lifted her chin. "Thank you, Ben, but it's all good. You need to go."

"No—"

Hazel rose from her chair. "Do you see that set of her jaw, Ben? She's decided, and there'll be no changing. Figure out the gala later, but you need to get home." She sniffed. "And cleaned up."

Despite the Muzak version of Jingle Bells playing in the background, defeat settled onto his shoulders. Ocean salt, vomit, sweat. He probably smelled worse than a dead fish.

"Come on, son. You're still looking a bit green too."

With the final blow to his confidence, he acquiesced and plodded out of the waiting room with Hazel.

Okay, Ginny. You've won this round, but I'm not giving up. I'll be back on my game with a settled stomach and a shirt without Santa hats. Get ready.

TAD RESTED PEACEFULLY on Ginny's couch, and another thank-you prayer formed in her mind. Although he'd lost almost a pint of blood and needed twelve stitches in his foot, he'd recover with a scar and a new tale to tell. She tried to pray away the anger she felt every time she remembered the race across the sound and poor Ben throwing up the whole time. She picked up her phone to text him, but Tad opened his eyes,

"Hey, sis." He shifted on the couch. "Thanks for coming to the rescue. Again."

She sipped her decaf coffee, dismissing his thanks. "The doc says you'll need to hang out a couple of days. Get your strength back."

"Yeah. How's Ben?"

She glanced at her phone. "Enjoying the gala probably."

"The gala? You're supposed to be there."

"I'm not going."

"You don't need to babysit me. I'm fine. Go."

"I'm not going."

"Yes, you are."

"It's too late."

"The mingle time's just started. Go get ready."

"I'm not going." Ginny clamped her jaw shut.

"Yes, you are 'cause you're not laying this on me. I'm sorry about the rescue, but you're back now. Get dressed and go. Celebrate with Ben. You taught him all he knows."

CHAPTER 13

*T*he throbbing in Ben's head banged like a timpani when the buffet of seafood and salads came into view at the gala. Would he ever feel like eating again? He asked for a ginger ale from the bartender and sipped on the bubbly liquid. The Christmas lights decorating the archway in the community center twinkled in time to the pattern pounding between his temples. He relieved his eyes of the dancing lights and surveyed the room. No Ginny. Would she show?

What a day. She barely spoke for the entire boat trip except to bark orders. Her brother was out of his head most of the time.

He'd expected to stay with her and be a friend, be a comfort, be a shoulder for her, but no. Instead, she pushed him into Hazel's care, dismissing him with a wave and a thank you.

Appreciating the string band's jazzy rendition of "We Three Kings," he took another sip before releasing the glass to a waiter's tray. His bed and a dark room beckoned him more than the anticipation of a thirty-dollar check. Turning toward the door, he stepped in front of a familiar face.

"Pastor Maron, Good to see you." It was good to see anything with the violent headache demanding all his attention.

"Good evening, son. I saw your name among the winners on the town's website. Congratulations for placing in the money."

"Yes, sir. Thank you. Honorable mention feels kind of good for my first competition. I can afford a few more Apple Uglies with my prize money."

"Ooh, they're just this side of sinful. I'm abstaining during December so I can enjoy my wife's Christmas cookies. Maybe the purse for next year's tournament can be a little healthier. Speaking of next year, how does the field look for our permanent bank manager? Any good prospects?"

"Felicia Combs mentioned two new résumés."

"Nice. Yours wouldn't be one of them, now, would it?"

Ben laughed. "Well—"

The crowd nudged him to his left.

Pastor Maron shifted with him. "I've heard good things about you, Ben. We'd be honored to count you as a neighbor. Hazel says she's asked you to play backup keyboard for us."

Commandeered better described Hazel's invitation to play when she'd discovered his piano skills. She didn't shy away from what she wanted, for sure.

GINNY SPOTTED BEN talking with Pastor Maron the instant she entered the room. Wearing a dark suit and paisley tie, his hair gelled in place, he proclaimed Mr. Big City. A cold sensation bloomed in her stomach, freezing tingly paths to her fingertips. She shivered.

He didn't belong in Hatteras any more than he belonged on her boat.

But Pastor Maron asked him to stay. She inched closer to the two as they shifted with the push of the crowd. A three-hundred-pound fisherman stepped between her and Ben's back, blocking her efforts to join their conversation as she strained to hear Ben's response about playing backup keyboard.

"The island's a beautiful place, no doubt. She's mentioned it, yes."

She braced herself. When he says, no, just keep smiling. There'll be plenty of time for other feelings later.

The linebacker fisherman wedged into an opening in the crowd, and Pastor Maron faced her. "Hello, Ginny. We were chatting about new prospects for the bank manager. I hope he'll apply for it."

Ben turned toward her, a tentative smile on his face.

Don't worry, Ben, I understand, and I'll help you out. "As much as we have to offer, I'm sure the sparkling city life is calling him back home, not to mention his family." She flashed a quick smile to Ben's jacket and switched her gaze to the pastor before Ben could confirm leaving. "The Christmas Classic Fishing Tournament is off to a great start, don't you think, Pastor?"

"Indeed. Next year we should be big enough for a sit-down dinner rather than a heavy appetizer party." He eyed the buffet table.

"From your mouth to God's ears," Ginny hoped her voice sounded normal. "Oh, there's Miss Edna. I need to speak to her, please excuse me." She touched Ben's sleeve and stepped away.

"Want a cup of spiced cider? I'll get you one."

"I'm good thanks," floated over her shoulder along with another pasted-on smile. Excellent. She'd made her appearance, let Ben know she understood about his leaving, kept her emotions under wraps. She'd inform Miss Edna the rod and reel she'd ordered for her granddaughter had arrived and then go home.

Telling Miss Edna wasn't imperative tonight—she called every day since she placed her order—but leaving the party was.

Mentally and physically exhausted from the day's drama, she didn't have energy to keep smiling at Ben with his leaving foremost in her mind.

She'd regroup before seeing him again, get her brain fully accepting a future without him.

CHAPTER 14

"So how was the big night? Do you like your trophy?" Josie teased over the phone.

"I got a check for thirty bucks. No trophy for honorable mention." By the time Ben had received Ginny's goodbye text, he'd searched the crowd for that clingy, swingy black dress for several minutes. Man, she always looked great, but tonight, even after the hours spent on the sound rescuing her brother, she could have lit up a red carpet anywhere. He'd have made sure she knew, if she hadn't left.

"So, when can we expect you? Please say Christmas Eve Eve."

"No can do. I'm working then so that I can have the whole long weekend. My co-workers are being more than generous with days off."

"It's not like you don't have days to take off. You're not a first-year hire, you know."

"Yeah. It's never a good look to come in and take days just because you can."

"So, sometime Christmas Eve?"

"I'll be there with bells on."

"Silver bells?"

"Funny, Josie. See you soon."

He checked the text box again. Nothing. He'd send one more and then call this day done.

> Hey. Got my check. Need some help spending it.
> Any ideas?

While waiting for a response, he took out his contacts, and heard one come through.

I'm sure you have great ideas. Congratulations again.

Hmm. Very non-committal.

> How's Tad?

Fine. Thanks. He'll be good as new before too long.

> How's your week look?

Swamped with last-minute shoppers.

> Gotcha. See you before I go home on Christmas Eve.

Okay. Good night.

GINNY SET aside her phone and fingered the black crepe of her fancy dress. She'd been home for hours, kicking off her heels but lingering in the dress that made her feel special, like Cinderella at the ball. The light in Ben's eyes when he saw her at the gala more than compensated for the money she'd spent on the full-price splurge.

She'd begun this friendship accepting its short-term status, but the fishing, the meals, the kissing—all those memory-making times had lolled her into a fantasy with Ben starring as lead. The daydream floundered a bit during the hang-gliding outing with the siblings' love sparkling all day and then again when Tad had arrived back in town.

Rescuing Tad, even though he was sober, gave Ben a glimpse of her not-so-sparkling sibling relationship while showcasing his kindness and strength despite a raging bout of seasickness. In case she still wondered if the friendship would grow into anything more, his magazine-cover look at the gala foghorned her foolishness.

Like Cinderella, she sighed, reality blanketing her own little corner on the island. Her brother slept in his old room down the hall. *Thank You, God, that he's on the mend. That he's still sober. Please keep him strong.*

Her life in Raleigh seemed as brief as the beam flickering every seven seconds from the lighthouse standing guard over the island.

Pastor Maron always exhorted his congregation to pray big to their big God. Fine. She took a breath. Okay, *Lord. I want him to stay but help me accept Your will.*

~

No YELLOW JEEP at the tackle shop. So much for surprising Ginny with a lunch invitation. He parked his car in the only available space and headed inside. She was right about last-minute shoppers. He caught Hazel's eye and waited while she rang up a shopper holding a list and a credit card.

"She's not here." Hazel said without looking at him.

"Yeah. I didn't see her Jeep. She's not at her house either. Do you know where she is?"

"Nope, but she's with Tad."

"Gotcha."

The shopper gathered the two bags of equipment and opened up the spot in front of Hazel.

"She hasn't texted me since Sunday night." And those weren't too forthcoming. He leaned in. "I'm driving home first thing tomorrow morning. I'd love to see her. Help a guy out, Hazel?"

"I'd love to, buddy, but she didn't tell me much. Just that she'd be out and sent that teenager over by the bait cooler to help me during this crunch time." She made a face at the lanky teen. "She left these two presents for you." She reached under the counter and pulled out two small packages. "One's for you. The other's for your sister."

That's how it's going to be? Exchanging presents by proxy? The seasickness must have really disappointed her.

He sighed. "Hers is in the car. I'll go get it. And yours too."

After a quick hug from Hazel for the Ringo Starr biography he'd found in the island's bookstore, Ben drove north on Highway12, scanning for a yellow Jeep. Not seeing one didn't deter him from continuing the search as he traveled onto the mainland into Columbia, his Christmas spirit absent from the westbound car.

CHAPTER 15

H ome for Christmas. Josie had dressed the house to a *T*. She'd unboxed the elementary school orna-ments, the fancy ones Mom gave them every year, the ones handed down from his grandparents. All of them hung on the shining tree.

The food ... delicious as usual ... the turnip greens with hot sauce alongside the beef tenderloin. Always an extravagance. Always worth every penny. Then the cookies. Dozens of cookies dressing up his great aunt's silver tray, and, of course, the apple and orange cake center stage on the dessert table with a side bowl of glazed pecans.

He grabbed a few pecans and tossed them in his mouth. The cinnamon and sugar tasted like home.

Every sight and smell proved Josie learned well from their mom. Perfect. But this year all the goodies, all the trimmings and smells and flickering lights did nothing to evoke the Christmas spirit in Ben's heart. His mind kept traveling back down Highway 12 to Hatteras.

What was Ginny doing? Did she think of him at all?

Josie's present.

He'd placed it under the Christmas tree with the others when he arrived home three hours ago, but it had shifted to the far side. He retrieved it, knocking off a shiny ball, and set it on a side table. He rehung the red ball and lost himself to more thoughts of Ginny.

"Hey, earth to Scrooge. Where've you been?" Josie entered the family room after saying good night to Ches. Heath and Sam had left too.

"Scrooge. A little harsh, don't you think? I came home bearing lots of gifts for all of you yahoos, and I get called Scrooge?"

"All right. You're not Scrooge, but where's your Christmas spirit? You've been in a mood all night. What gives?"

"Just tired after the drive, Jo."

"That may be part of it, but there's something else. Or rather someone else." She studied him.

He focused on the Christmas tree, ignoring her comment and her scrutiny. Thoughts about his job in Charlotte, his three months on the Outer Banks with Ginny pushed everything else aside.

"I saw the way you watched her Thanksgiving weekend. You're smitten with her."

"Smitten?" He turned toward her with an arched brow.

"It's a good word."

"For a history professor."

She chewed on the inside of her cheek. "You're taking the job, aren't you?"

His mouth dropped open. "I haven't made any commitments—"

"Out loud maybe, but you're thinking about staying. I can see it in your eyes."

"Okay, Miss Dog-With-a-Bone." He looked over her head at the wooden Advent calendar they'd had since childhood and sighed. "I've considered offering to stay longer. The incoming résumés aren't exactly lighting up the search committee."

Josie's chin trembled, prompting a hug from her brother. "What about the promotion?"

"Yeah, I've a lot to sort out. The promotion would be great, but I like what I'm doing on the island." The gift on the side table caught his attention. "Hey. You've got another present." He handed it to her. "It's from Ginny."

"Sweet." Josie ripped the ribbon and the wrapping off in one tear. Opening the box, she gasped. "A conch shell. She gave me a conch shell. Like she promised." She flattened her lips. "You've got to go back, Ben."

"What?"

"You have to go back."

"I am. Monday."

"No. You have to go back tomorrow." She caught her bottom lip with her teeth, then sighed. "Spend at least part of Christmas with her. Wait." She turned and ran away from him, stomping all the way up the steps. Five minutes later, she carried a small, square box, dropped it into a tossed-aside gift bag and stuffed tissue paper from the used pile she'd refold sometime after Christmas. She handed him the package. "Here. Take this to her."

"You got a present for her in five minutes?"

"It helps that I'm back in my parents' house. No problem finding my treasure box." She pushed it toward him. "Give it to her on Christmas, please."

"Josie."

"I'll move breakfast to eight. Sam can grouse all he wants. You'll eat fast and be on the road by eight thirty. You'll be back on Hatteras by early afternoon."

His heart rate ticked up. Emotion mushroomed in his chest. "Well, if you want her to have this present on Christmas Day."

"She absolutely has to have it tomorrow." Josie grinned at him.

He grinned back. "I can FaceTime with Mom and Dad from there, right?"

"Maybe have her join you."

"You think?" He laughed.

"There he is. You finally made it home for Christmas, Ben."

"Want some hot chocolate before we start the movie?" Ginny stretched and rose from the couch. "Or are you still stuffed?"

Her brother clicked the remote and pulled up a streaming service. "Sounds good. Hey, thanks for including me with your Christmas lunch. It's good to be home, sis. Hazel seems to be warming up to me too."

"She loves you. Give her time to come around." Her new slippers from Tad cushioned her feet like pillows as she padded into the kitchen. She poured milk into her Santa mug and, just to tease him, poured some into the Grinch one.

Crossing to the pantry, she glanced out the window. Sunlight glinted off a car pulling into the driveway. Did Hazel forget something? She surveyed the counter tops. Nothing. She glanced out the window again, her stomach dropping to her feet.

Ben.

He left yesterday, and he's back today. What? Sucking in a long breath, she held it as he walked up the path to the house. She released the breath with a prayer for help and strength and for her mouth to stop smiling so big.

Calm down, girl. You don't know why he's here.

But does it matter? He's back and here for Christmas even though he'd already left her present. She twisted the bracelet on her wrist, a silver braided chain with an Ichthys symbol clasp and one dangling aquamarine piece of sea glass. Hazel had made googly eyes when she saw it this morning.

He rapped on the front door. She breathed a steadying prayer.

"I'll get it." She jogged to the foyer, finger brushing her hair. Opening the door, she mirrored the tentative smile on his face.

"Hey."

"Hey back."

"I hope you don't mind me crashing Christmas."

"But you went home."

"Christmas Eve was great. Then Josie made me leave this morning."

"What?"

He peered behind her. "Could I come in, please?"

"Of course." Shaking her head, she stepped back. "You caught me off guard. Want some hot chocolate?"

Ben glanced at the two mugs. "Hazel?"

"Left a little while ago. Tad's queuing up a movie."

"Feel like a walk? I need to move around after the drive."

Tad appeared in the hall. "What's up, Ben? Merry Christmas."

"Merry Christmas. It's been a good one so far." They shook hands.

"Hey, man." Tad dipped his head and rubbed the side of his nose. "I never thanked you for helping my sister. I really appreciate it."

"Well, if you mean throwing up the whole time—"

"Naw, man. She said you helped get me in the boat. I was out of it."

"It's all good."

She set the Grinch mug in the microwave. "Your hot chocolate will be ready in a bit. We're going for a walk, okay?"

"Right. I can manage the microwave. Take your jacket. I see white caps out there. The sun's out, but the wind's up."

Ben lifted her jacket from the hall tree and held it for her. As

87

she slipped her arm through the sleeve, he touched her wrist. "Hey. You're wearing it."

"Uh-huh. Thank you, by the way." She draped the sea glass charm on her index finger, let it go and shrugged her jacket on both shoulders. "Hazel oohed and aahed over it."

"What did you do?"

"I put it on." She smiled and lost herself in his green eyes with the gold flecks.

Without planning, they headed for the dock behind her house.

"That reminds me. Josie sent you something." He pulled a gift bag from an inside pocket and handed it to her.

"Oh, that's so sweet." She stopped and turned to him. "She didn't have to."

"She loved the conch shell. I think it tipped things in favor of my early return. Did you really save it all these years? Or was it a different one?"

"I almost threw it back in the ocean, but I changed my mind and kept it. Who knows why? I never expected to see you again." She peeked inside the bag and drew out a square box. Opening it, she chuckled. "It's a friendship bracelet." One end whipped in the breeze when she held it for him to see.

"Safe guess it's twenty years old too." He laughed. "Hot pink, purple, lime—her favorite colors back in the day."

She extended her arm toward him. "Could you tie it for me?"

"Are you sure you want it on the same wrist? It'll have to compete with that bracelet Hazel loves."

"I love it too. I love both of them. They mean … a lot. Trust me."

Silence accompanied them to the end of the dock. During their last dock visit, he'd kissed her for the first time. Her heart raced at the thought.

Ben pulled up the collar of her jacket. "Tad was right. The wind's strong out here today."

Hair swirled around her face. Catching a lock, he smoothed it behind her ear. His thumb found her earlobe. Her insides melted, warmth rippling through her body despite the relentless December wind.

"Why'd you pull away last week?" He scanned her face. "I thought we were—"

Unlocking her gaze from his, she focused on the seagulls soaring on the current.

Gently, he guided her chin back to center with his index finger. "Tell me. What went wrong? It's my lack of seaworthiness, right?"

She laughed at the crazy thought, but his face showed concern and a curious bit of hurt, not levity. He stepped back.

"Ben, no." She grabbed the edges of his jacket. "Tad's right. You helped me so much. I couldn't have gotten him on the boat. Your presence meant a lot. I was scared, and your prayer settled me. Got me going again."

He frowned. "Did I pray out loud?"

"Short and to the point, but it worked."

"Then what? You didn't deny pulling away. What made you?"

The last time she explained her feelings, darkness gave her courage. This time … *God, help me out here, please.* "Your life is back in Charlotte with your family. Mine is here, at the shop, helping Tad. He's on his way to fine, but …" She shrugged.

"Seeing you all spiffed up in your suit helped me remember our places. Helped me get ready for when you go back to Charlotte for good."

His fingers slid along her jaw, down the side of her neck. "What if I could stay here longer?"

She shivered and quelled the immediate urge to latch on to the lapels of his jacket. "What does that mean exactly?"

∾

LIGHT-HEARTED FEELINGS WHIRLING in his heart, Ben cleared his throat. "It means I'm considering accepting a long-term position here."

Her eyes widened. "Long term as in how long?"

"Six months or more."

A tiny smile perked up the corners of her mouth.

"I have to get some things settled back home, but it could allow me to rent something more than one room at Teachy's. He drew her toward him. "I think we have something interesting happening between us, and maybe we should explore it some more. What do you think? Should I accept the position?"

Her smile grew. "I think, yes. Please accept it."

"Good." Heat thumped in his chest. "Because you still have to show me Ocracoke."

"Right. Will do. And we haven't been surfing yet either."

"Speaking of surfing, Yancy Buress's eightieth birthday is Old Christmas. Would she hate us if we threw her a party?"

"You can tell her."

He laughed and kissed her temple. "I hear the turtle season is pretty spectacular." He whispered near her ear. "And you have that hang-gliding coupon."

"Mmm. I love a coupon." She wrapped her arms around his waist. "You really need more practice fishing too."

"You want me to do better than honorable mention?" He trailed kisses along her cheek. "See, I have to stay longer."

"This is turning out to be a great Christmas."

"Maybe I can make it even better." And he lowered his lips to hers.

ABOUT THE AUTHOR

Hope Toler Dougherty holds a Master's degree in English and taught at East Carolina University and York Technical College. Her publications include four novels, *Irish Encounter* and *Mars...With Venus Rising*, *Rescued Hearts*, and *Forever Music* as well as nonfiction articles. A member of ACFW and RWA, she lives in North Carolina. She and her husband enjoy visits with their two daughters and twin sons. Visit her at hopetolerdougherty.com.

FOREVER SERIES

Forever Music

Book One in the Forever Series

by Hope Toler Dougherty

A battered heart needs healing.

A community needs rescuing.

A chartered course needs redirecting.

College history instructor, Josie Daniels is good at mothering her three brothers, volunteering in her community, and getting over broken hearts, but meeting aloof, hotshot attorney Ches Windham challenges her nurturing, positive-thinking spirit.

Josie longs to help Ches find his true purpose, but as his hidden talents and true personality emerge. Will she be able to withstand his potent charms, or will she lose her heart in the process?

A rising star in his law firm, Ches Windham is good at keeping secrets.

He's always been the good son, following his father's will to become an attorney and playing the game for a fast track to partnering with a law firm. Lately, though his life's path has lost whatever luster it had—all because of his unlikely, and unacceptable, friendship with Josie. He struggles between the life he's prepared for and the one calling to him now. Opposing his father has never been an option, and spending time with Josie can't be one. The more he's with her, however, the more he wants to be.

When a crisis tarnishes his golden future and secrets are revealed, Ches is forced to reexamine the trajectory of his life. Will he choose the path his father hammered out for him or the path that speaks to his heart?

Forever Home

Book Three in the Forever Series

by Hope Toler Dougherty

With a fulfilling job and a home of her own, former foster child, Merritt Hastings, relishes her stable, respectable life. Dreaming for more is a sure way for heartache. When a contested will turns her world upside down, she must revaluate what's important to her, what's worth fighting for, and what's worth sacrificing.

Patience has never been Sam Daniels' strong suit with his history of acting quickly and asking questions later, and he's ready for changes in his life...now. Too bad the plans for acquiring a radio station didn't include a contract. Now he's out of a job, out of a radio station, and out of prospects.

While his life is in flux, at least he can help Merritt steady hers, or will he rush in and overstep ...again?

Will the sparks flying between these two opposites lead to a happily-ever-after or heartbreak for both?

Irish Encounter

After almost three years of living under a fog of grief, Ellen Shepherd is ready for the next chapter in her life. Perhaps she'll find adventure during a visit to Galway. Her idea of excitement consists of exploring Ireland for yarn to feature in her shop back home, but the adventure awaiting her includes an edgy stranger who disrupts her tea time, challenges her belief system, and stirs up feelings she thought she'd buried with her husband.

After years of ignoring God, nursing anger, and stifling his grief, Payne Anderson isn't ready for the feelings a chance encounter with an enchanting stranger evokes. Though avoiding women and small talk has been his pattern, something about Ellen makes him want to seek her —and God again.

Can Ellen accept a new life different than the one she planned? Can Payne release his guilt and accept the peace he's longed for? Can they surrender their past pain and embrace healing together, or will fear and doubt ruin their second chance at happiness?

~

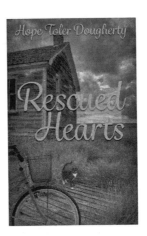

Rescued Hearts

Mary Wade Kimball's soft spot for animals leads to a hostage situation when she spots a briar-entangled kitten in front of an abandoned house. Beaten, bound, and gagged, Mary Wade loses hope for escape.

Discovering the kidnapped woman ratchets the complications for undercover agent Brett Davis. Weighing the difference of ruining his three months' investigation against the woman's safety, Brett forsakes his mission and helps her escape the bent-on-revenge brutes following behind. When Mary Wade's safety is threatened once more, Brett rescues her again. This time, her personal safety isn't the only thing in jeopardy. Her heart is endangered as well.

~

Scrivenings
PRESS
Quench your thirst for story.
www.ScriveningsPress.com

Stay up-to-date on your favorite books and authors with our free e-newsletters.

ScriveningsPress.com

Made in the USA
Columbia, SC
19 August 2022

65605346R00059